A Wander Within Wonder

Penshurst Publishing (Books)   First Edition—October 2020

Author — F. Bradley Reaume

ISBN # 978-1-7770810-1-0

Introduction

In its original incarnation, 'Wander Within Wonder' was a verse narrative, telling the story of Endell, an everyman who lives an epic life, attaining all his goals, but who doesn't stop to consider his ultimate purpose.

Originally written in verse, it took well more than a decade to complete in between my other responsibilities. I had taken on the task as a challenge and a way to improve my prose composition.

I believed that working through short verse pieces, between a few lines and a few stanzas, would help me sharpen my skills to be a more effective writer of prose. Verse does not waste words and requires a precision on placement and word selection that can only benefit prose composition.

But 'Wander Within Wonder' had grown in length and with it came a much larger conception of what I wanted it to be. I shelved the project despite being deeply into the narrative. What I had conceived required a dedication to the task of keeping the story at the forefront of my mind that was beyond what I could manage given my other responsibilities.

After some time without any forward progress I decided that if I was ever to get past 'Wander Within Wonder' and free myself for other tasks, I needed to finish it. So I chose to scale down my plan and compress the story.

Ultimately my goal was novel length fiction, but I resolved to complete 'Wander Within Wonder' before taking on that task.

And so I conceived of a much shorter version of the story of 'Wander Within Wonder', rationalizing that the original vision was much too long and would necessarily belabour the points I was trying to make.

Laziness winning out, I was able to finish the story and the verse to produce the 3,000 line finished narrative poem. It is written in three parts, each of 100 stanzas, 10 lines in length, predominately in iambic rhyming couplets of varying length.

The variations are used to dramatic effect and to make the whole more readable as its function does not become bogged down by a slavering dedication to the form.

I hope the result is pleasing.

I have seen in most lengthy narrative poems that in order to advance the story satisfactorily it is universally acknowledged that the form must be broken from time to time. And yet, in re-reading it, the best parts are bursts of verse that stay on the point of form, while producing what seems to me to be flashes of wit, wisdom or insight.

I cannot imagine matching the length of some of literature's most lengthy verse tales which make 'Wander Within Wonder's length seem a mere trifle. Nor could I dedicate the necessary colossal requirement of time to create such a work. To those who have, I acknowledge the difficulty.

Now, versifying is not something in the early 21st century that garners one much praise or notoriety. So I have quietly sat on my printed version of 'Wander Within Wonder', which was collected into a volume with a dozen other much shorter pieces, not show-ing it to very many people, nor mentioning its existence.

Quietly, for some time, I have wondered myself, if a prose version of the story might give the verse itself a little life. And so here it is, the long poem Wander Within Wonder, printed anew with a few edits to fix transcription issues, and coupled with a prose version.

I must confess that in preparing this publication I have found much wanting, primarily in diction and precision. However, I have also delighted myself with the depth of the narrative and the value of the story and its form. There is much here to contem-plate, even if the details are a bit hazy in the function of the verse.

I hope you will enjoy the story. I hope you will take time to read the verse and at least admire the attempt. I hope that students of writing will find some value in having both versions side by each.

And above all, I hope beyond hope, that it "adds weight to my sodden grave," and isn't entirely without merit.

Brad Reaume, 2020

A Wander within Wonder

Canto One - Endell's Song

The Argument

Though oft I sing of silent, simple night,
Sometimes still I speak of dazzling daylight,
I wonder of speeding time and wide space,
I watch the seasons gravitate from grace.
Though I in thought when reigns and rains fall,
When red roses bloom and cardinals call,
Sing I the same, I cannot creation change,
One's work of ages, though be it so strange.
I comment on the full wonder of things,
From the largest to the least that life brings.

Past these I worry still of dreaded death,
Of time without measure, alive without breath.
Can faith reduce fright of black beyond?
Can reason secure hope white light will dawn?
I think of tomorrow yet live for today,
And I wish I could wander through time to stay.
Answers I would have and things I would see,
I could know the sky and talk with a tree.
Yet I speak of hell, and so often do,
It is heaven I hope to be going to.

Oh! Muse of the moment, magic I crave,
Verse to add weight to my sodden grave.
Of peaceful and green pregnant lands sang I,
Of lovers' hopes and of lovers' soft sighs.
With lyric and lament to labor pain,
To happy times and dancing in rain.
Ere now, standing at the word forge I held,
Crudely attempted, twisted verse, to weld.
My dues are now coffered, a muse to seek,
I bow to your poetry when I speak.

Of man and god, divinity in each,
Of power and possessions I hope to teach.
This condition of life confronts us all,
And even through darkest death, always shall.
Enter into our world, everything wanting,
Leave with nothing and all earth on a string.
Of time and trouble for truth and beauty,
To find a purpose, to struggle with duty.
Of all men and each with race and creed,
To all those men who worship greed: be freed.

In The Beginning

A noble figure lay silent on the lawn,
Full green he was and misty with the dawn.
Small stream soundless, lay close by mighty hand,
Willow and poplar, shade the misty land.
Temperate the day, yet cool the dark night,
A land of pure pleasure, a land of fright.
'Twas mythic and magical, never the same,
The world was still young, so rather untame.
Wonders were everyday, though singular,
And the rumors of them, traveled far.

The figure a man, though he naked be,
Silent like sleep, he lay shaded by tree.
As the sun crept up an ocean blue sky,
The tide of light swept shade away, sun high.
The figure blinked and stretched to feel,
If soft green grass and the bright sun were real.
Mist hung above a meander of water,
Most burned away as the day became hotter.
The figure sat still as the earth around,
       "I am Endell, lost and finally found."

On his feet, he felt his supple sinews,
And marveled at each muscle he used.
The strength, the keen precision of power,
He knew he was not intended to cower.
In a flush of pride he sped about,
He could run with felt fury and without doubt.
His body he remembered and knew,
Yet of other memories he had no clue.
But now he knew his mission in this place,
To make his name as fearsome as his face.

Down to the dancing, soundless stream he ran,
Singing wordless like some pipeless Pan,
      "Running water runs away from something,
      And always enters new lands loitering.
      I want to face the fire first, so upstream,
      What is water running from? Evil, I deem."
With a wide step and stride he started away,
And came on a man once dressed in grey.
Then Endell knew he was naked, so he,
Fashioned a covering from a tree.

He spied the man's clothing close at hand,
    "They will do," thought he, "though they be bland."
Endell freed the steed and stole away slow,
Leaving the farm cart to lessen the blow.
Now provisioned and horsed by knave,
The horse begged a name which he soon gave.
    "Garland be bold," he stroked on its mane,
    "And from my commands do never refrain."
The steed with a sound stirred Endell's heart,
This was no nag for a farmer and cart.

Galloping mare matched master in grey,
Garland stately, rural rider the stray.
Farmer's dull clothes, coarse with good care,
Many patches and stops but nary a tear.
They rode 'till sun stared down dewed horizon,
Light lingering on treetops ere night won.
Dawn spread the new day out for the eye,
Grasslands behind, a vast forest was nigh.
Endell entranced, stood arms wide in awe,
The ominous, ancient wood, all he saw.

Though Endell knew not of this ancient wood,
He saw that no light entered that should.
Each tree gave soft glow according to age,
From smallest sapling to great hoary sage.
Like minor moon glow gave the oldest tree,
Alone or in sunlight, impossible to see.
Yet deep in the forest the only light,
Never bright by day, never dark at night.
Many streams and vales meander the floor,
Direction a maze says the oldest lore.

Known as Garadreium Wood since days dimmest,
Where few men would wander time as a guest.
Still, some are said to travel its ways,
Some for pure purpose and others as strays.
'Tis told in the center of the wild wood,
Lay an oracle to tell evil or good.
This teller a pool, named Mithomere,
Your thoughts in reflection, dreams yours to steer.
Yet beware the ripple across your scene,
Saps your attention to change what you mean.

There are many paths and forks to follow,
And roads whose destinations are hollow.
Many creatures will see and be seen,
Who in wild Garadreium have always been.
Which is a wild witch and which a true troll,
Some wanting money and others your soul.
Beware of the woodland, all is awake,
Silent and stifling awaiting mistake.
From foul evil to wonder oh so fair,
In the marches of Garadreium, beware.

Endell mounted Garland, his gentle mare,
And entered the forest with utmost care.
They followed the river not the path,
Inviting the forest to release its wrath.
Once in the forest and out of sun sight,
The brambles on the bank became a blight,
Till the mare could not move forward or back.
Endell dismounted, and with a stick, hacked.
Slowly the vines, were slashed and torn out,
But in from the river, the only way out.

Their path and purpose, the river, they lost,
Endell soon saw with fate they had crossed.
A path presented an easier way,
For fools to find fortune without delay.
Narrow the manner and not often used,
>"Forward to a formal road," Endell mused,
>"Or back beyond forest fresh memory,
>To die, in some flash of mythical glory?"
Endell stopped a shiver with wonder,
Why was his being, pulled asunder?

Garland could sense his master's unease,
Like the sudden shift of blowing breeze.
To a confident canter he changed,
So spirits could rise up and fortunes range.
Further afield with interest they seek,
All paths corners no longer made meek.
With the glow of the great mythic hero,
They sped seeking savage, faithless foul foe.
Branches were broken by on both sides,
Of the path, by the horse and the man who rides.

Sleep seems to escape from the forest,
Yet no traveler worried for right rest.
Still red roses and white, and daisies rise,
Orchids bloom, lilies grow and vines disguise.
The forest fosters fair scenes to deny,
The hard horror from those destined to die.
From flowers and trees and glades of green,
To unnatural eyes and the Faery Queen,
The Garadreium Wood has all complete,
More than a match for Endell to greet.

The path opened on a wider way,
A pavilion with lone maid who did say,
>"Glory and gold or giants greed occur,
>Which way wouldst thou go gladly, brave sir?
>Three questions can you ask to gain some clue,
>But one query I answer with heart true."
The maid fell silent as stone, and as hard,
An evil fate had sentenced her to guard,
The very road she had faltered upon.
Now Garland and Endell to danger drawn.

The soft breath of breeze sounded the leaves,
In high trees only the thrush believes.
>"I crave not safety with warm wee fire,
>And deal I not with a two-thirds liar.
>I shall venture to east, right along the road,
>To the rising life-giver, light sowed.
>With likewise license I shall rise to greet,
>All honorable men I chance to meet."
He reigned his steed and started east,
Wondering, would he find, monster or priest?

>"Stop sir and save me," the damsel screamed,
Though to her, under spell, it soft seemed.
>"Once a soul has defied the foul fate,
>It be free to flee the forest as bait.
>While I run to the edge of the wood,
>All things evil will give chase that could.
>Escort me please from this dreaded spot,
>For evil moves and my fear is fraught."
>"Nay lady," spoke a grim and strong Endell,
>"For evil I look, to face horror fell."

His face brightened a bit, "Yes you stay,
Find me the fight and I'll take you away."
She meekly agreed and climbed the steed,
   "Find strong defense and of my tale take heed."
Endell laughed, his face creased in smile,
   "Lady, your fate is but my first trial,
   I hope far beyond this harrowing test,
   Although I am not sure for what I quest."
   "How will you win when you are weaponless,
   Carrying no armor and in farmer's dress?"

   "That bridge shall I cross at proper point,
   When the threat is before and the terror joint."
Evening was closing, they stopped under tree,
And readied for what the evil might be.
A monster with jaws or a giant tall,
A black cloaked rider with a careful crawl.
The maiden slept sound her head on a pillow,
A root covered with leaves of the willow.
As dawn flecked the flora with morning,
The maiden awoke and trumpeted warning.

The root with the night changed to suffice,
Wild willow to trap her neck like a vise.
   "Evil has come," she cried when she woke,
And even with those words began to choke.
Endell leapt to the task thrusting a branch,
In the space between root and ground, his chance.
A rock wedge and little lever made,
A touch of force and the root paid.
A might crack and the root split asunder,
Freeing the maid and Endell to wonder.

"Take heed my words brave fool, the evil grows,
And worse it follows close and it knows."
"If that is the worst your dire curse will dare,
I feel safe and so should you damsel fair."
"Take it not light I swear marked we are,
I must escape the forest, yet 'tis far."
Endell threw his head back and laughed loud.
"I should go, I fear men who are that proud,"
Said she, as he smiled a broad beam,
"Still not much more than a farmer you seem."

Garland had finished his graze of day,
To return into this domestic fray.
At last retort, he gave a great snort,
And a stamp, displeasured at the report.
Despite appearances he knew their road,
Was to be long and hard with heavy load.
Yet they would endure to win wide renown,
In the farms, in the cities, in the towns.
He had found his calling, a great war horse,
And with Endell he would be a fierce force.

The maid turned to the steed and smiled,
She knew his mind, he saw, and was beguiled.
They rode from the willow without trouble,
But soon encountered it in double.
Two huge beasts with long snouts of teeth,
Heavy hide like armor except underneath.
They ran on four legs and walked on two,
Rose to frighten and stayed low to view.
Their eyes set on either side of the head,
Depth lost, vast visual angles instead.

A knight armed with sword, rushes the pair,
But Endell, weaponless, had no chance there.
He dropped off the steed at a safe distance,
Found a few stones, more deadly than lance.
The first found an eye the second the same,
And two one-eyed beasts had Endell to blame.
Both backed away to preserve mere defeat,
Blindness is death, thus explaining retreat.
The maid had worked a weapon full quick,
She fashioned a ready sharp stick.

Endell was sure where his destiny lay,
That he would find fight no matter which way.
Now with a weapon, a rough wooden lance,
He felt full sure fate would give him a chance.
To fight for a moral and worthwhile gain,
To win without worry, to inflict pain.
The ride was a pleasure for Endell's thought,
But the maid felt both cornered and caught.
Deeper through the wood they traveled true,
Facing nothing worse than the morning dew.

The immediate world such a simple place,
From familiar gardens of informal grace,
The solitary tree of sleep's story,
Grows as slowly as a child's memory.
Around each turn in the road eyes widen,
One with a cringe, anytime could be when,
The other leaning into challenge,
Like a man seeking running revenge.
He became bolder, each step a strike,
She worried further with each footfall hiked.

"My fair lady, I am most mannerless,
Speak with soft speed your name ere I guess."
He closed his eyes yet bore a grin,
She wistfully whispered, "Evelyn."
He laughed, and still harder at her shock,
"I should have guessed, and would," he mocked.
Though she knew he thought himself clever,
Turning the tide became her endeavor.
"And of names, dear sir, do you have one?"
"Not that you know, 'tis Endell, not a pun."

"Still 'tis the name I gained at birth,
Which recent events have changed to mirth.
Rather a rarefied attempt at wit,
But then if you wear it, it should fit.
No, Endell is majestic beyond you,
With your farmers' clothes and homemade brew.
Yet call you it I will, your wish and goal,
Still, I see the day you will answer to Arrol."
They plodded along toward the next turn,
Which hid an evil terrible and stern.

Nothing had they encountered since morn,
And nothing yet faced had they not borne.
The sight caused Garland to halt in stride,
There lay before them a river wide.
Too far and fast for bridge to span,
Where raging eddies of red water ran.
Too swift to ford, so stood a ferryman,
With a flat bottomed boat, 'Lady Anne'.
He was old but not of wrinkled look,
His skin was fair, his eyes a moving brook.

"Say you! Man! Can we cross yonder torrent?"
"By whose will, for what purpose are you sent?"
"I and my steed to find a destiny here,
And young Evelyn I protect from evil near."
"Strange and strong words for a farmer to speak,
Still in the wood there is no normal freak.
I shall take you across but do not stray,
The red enchanted river can delay,
Your crossing of my employer's realm.
A single drop in place, will overwhelm."

They entered the boat and with one stroke,
Of the ferryman's pole the quick current broke.
A calm on the water, smooth as glass,
Caused wide wonder and no words to pass.
A green fish crested the smooth surface,
But the splashed water did well miss.
Yet the maid moved to the boat's far side,
As the fish jumped again splashing wide.
Then once more a mighty leap with flips,
The tail flicked a drop on Evelyn's lips.

Her eyes grew wide and she stood shock still,
And slowly fell backwards against her will.
Nothing could she move, not even to cry,
A swift sweep of fear, produced a sigh.
Endell spun around and saw her fall in,
He went to dive for her but saw her grin.
She floated like a board, face finding sky,
He fished her in and found her clothing dry,
Soon as he pulled her from the surface,
She clung to him and gave him a kiss.

The river ran, enraged at the theft,
Swirled and sped throwing them right and left.
They were carried far down the swollen stream,
Deeper and deeper into Garadreium.
Faintly the wind carried a falling roar,
They knew they would die or get to shore.
A mist thickened the air all around,
And though Evelyn screamed they heard no sound,
Save the river crashing beyond the last bend.
They seemed destined to ride to the end.

The swollen river gave them but slim hope,
But Endell fastened the boat to a rope.
As the current swept round the last full turn,
They were pushed to far bank, first the stern.
Endell in earnest gazed at the trees,
Waiting a chance his moment to seize.
Then within reach a sturdy open branch,
He knew it was their one single chance.
The edge was quite clear and so a scan,
A table cloth of tree leaves covered the land.

Looping the rope over a hanging limb,
They stopped the boat at cataract's rim.
They pulled on the twine and beat the current,
But by the time they were safe all were spent.
        "The water will have some further effect,
        One never knows which darkness will select.
        Enchantments can be deep or very light,
        On the maid there seems no sign of despite.
        Watch her wary for strange advance,
        From aggression to a zombie's trance."

"You seem well acquainted with enchantment,
Who is your lord and why were you sent,
Out of your realm to be a ferryman?"
"Well, it was not in the original plan.
I was a noble and lived at king's court,
Engaged to marry with king's support,
His daughter, beautiful and heir to throne.
The king had favored but me alone.
Then a terrible accident took place,
At the ferry I fell from king's grace.

"I was with the girl as we traveled,
Across yon river with much rain swelled.
In my care was she, and had been before,
But of the river, Mead, I knew no lore.
As we crossed the terrible torrent . . .
Oh God! Of my folly I do repent . . .
I calmed the surface, like today,
And one single large wave swept her away.
I dove in to save her, not knowing fear,
For she was my love, ever so dear.

"I loved her as man never felt,
Before this pounding heart, my future dealt.
Perhaps it is the way, retribution,
I pay for easy, simple solutions,
To my problems, in the court and when out,
And of my position I had no doubt.
Yet cast my eyes down, humble was I,
When I spoke with the king, or she was nigh.
She carried herself like an autumn stream,
Slowly, with grace, the water with dream.

"Oft times she simply floated past me,
And I, captured by her sight, could see,
What wonder that life held, from largest to least.
From the first time she spoke, love never ceased.
More than mere song from tuneless nightingale,
It spoke to me removing my heart's veil.
She was like all things you always treasure,
Like those things that are well beyond measure.
But lose her did I, my awful found fate,
Condemned to grow old but never to date.

"I must stay ferryman and bear my cross,
I stay young so to always feel the loss.
Others rescued me from the water,
But never found Lady Anne, king's daughter.
I was enchanted and in trance deep,
Before they saw the secondary sleep.
The red river has my life in its grip,
For the trance returns without daily sip,
Of the river which caused my full woe.
At king's decree, I was forced to row.

"'Tis how I came to spend my life here,
And yes, I weep and shed many tears,
Not for myself, but rather, Lady Anne,
Beloved, I stay beside brook span,"
Said the sorrowful figure to the stream,
Eyes so moist of tears they did gleam.
They sat in silence some minutes until,
The ferryman's mind was shook with chill.
"We are within bounds of the king,
Better to go than be caught loitering."

The company took leave of their guide,
After escorting him to where hope died.
     "To the king." While Garland clawed the air,
But Evelyn was settling back to despair.
Would evil follow them into the realm?
Then two men with sturdy steeds, sword and helm,
Blocked the road and signaled halt.
     "Well foul tiller, might it be your fault?"
     "Might what? I seek the king to gain his leave,
     To travel this realm my fortune to cleave."

     "Did you pass the ford or come another way?"
     "The river was rough yet we won the day,
     Though well down the stream were we before crossing,
     The full tale is not very engrossing."
     "The ferryman was with you in your plight?"
     "We left him at the ford to set things right,
     Nodded Endell, "and he pointed us the road,
     On which we should find king's abode."
     Three days said he, should enable us arrive,
     As long as we manage to stay alive."

     "Times have changes since he knew the land,
     The kingdom is more powerful and grand.
     This road is quite safe, save from one,
     A ruffian roams and has full run,
     Of all the crown lands, he never leaves,
     Protected lands, so everyone believes.
     So peaceful this realm, he can forage,
     Unmolested as the earner of a wage.
     We release you to travel to the king,
     But show care, lest you feel either sting."

They went on west now for the turns turned them,
Toward the setting sun like a blazing gem.
The forest had opened to tilled fields,
Where farming folk might have a hoe to wield.
And the best weapon, a free mug o beer,
Where armies on march are considered queer,
Where the king lives comfortably near,
But on a fabled gold throne without peer.
Evelyn began to relax and release,
The absence of evil brought forth peace.

They talked with friendly faces they met,
And stopped to sleep once the sun set.
They entered into a broad valley,
Carved by the slow river Orvalee.
The king's castle shone by the water course,
Though not far away with Garland their horse.
Upstream lay the town around the king's court,
Which rose high but with walls down to a port.
The keep walls golden so they shone with the sun,
With bright light the castle Orvalee would stun.

Down, down to the valley floor ran the path,
Which would carry the company to wrath.
A bridge carried the road, current clear,
And there stood Silas astride his mount, Fear.
Highwayman some say, though other disagree,
Such cruelty they had never known could be.
A thief who would beat you if you were weak,
Had never been seen, save by the meek,
Upon whom he preyed with size and strength.
The king vowed to go to any length.

A boy but fourteen summers seen, came to
The bridge to sell vegetables few,
In the town beyond. But Silas held ground,
Between boy and bridge, and all around.
The boy advanced to flight or fight,
Knowing his goods lost once in Silas' sight.
The giant stood astride his fearful steed,
Silent, while the boy bowed to plead.
      "Do not hurt me brave Sir when you steal,
      I am damned to revenge 'fore I heal."

So Silas laughed long and laughed loud,
For he was sure of glory and full proud.
      "If I even think long, people will try,
      When they hear, to scare me with such a lie,
      But if I crush this insolent soul,
      My reputation will take no toll!"
He reined his horse and reared in wrath,
      "Before your foul lies hound me, you hath
      Better prepare for death so no vengeance,
      Can you visit upon me or dispense."

With that he drew his sword charging the boy,
Who leaped behind his cart to annoy,
The murderous giant whose first swing missed.
He ran up the broad bridge shaking his fist.
Silas, determined to make short time,
Of this trouble to get on with his crime.
Fear faced the bridge, black its breath,
And its rider an instrument of death.
With a spur the horse pounced like a pall,
But the boy escaped over the wall.

The soft grass below sloped to the stream,
Which flowed deep, yet like a thick cream.
Silas was livid he could not catch,
A mere child who had eluded his snatch.
The attacker recovered and followed
The boy, while ignoring his prize, the load.
The child was secreted now in a cave,
Full confident the situation less grave.
But if the highwayman found him out,
The only true end would be the boy's rout.

"Come child," cooed Silas, "where might you be?"
The company arrived there to see,
A pony and full farm cart all alone,
Save a man trampling brush and turning stone,
Some way down the river, searching it seemed,
And babbling and cooing as in a dream.
"Sir, might this pony cart belong to you?"
Endell shouted, "Will you sell what you grew?"
And a little voice called, "Tis mine,
The cart. The large man to theft does incline."

"Sir, is this charge correct and spoken true?
Who owns this voice that is hidden from view?"
The boy appeared some distance away,
From the giant who wished for a fray.
He charged the boy who ducked again.
"Sir, with sword I must demand you refrain,
From swinging at the child until you explain,
Why the bridge bodes better with blood stain."
"Stranger you aren't armed enough to,
Enforce your will. Be gone into the blue."

With that turned back to terrible task,
Attacking now without attempt to mask,
His murderous intentions on the child.
Endell leapt from Garland, angry wild,
He began to throw things from the full cart,
At the giant, while the boy did his part.
Silas turned to fight his new found foe,
Rodney ran to remove horse and cargo.
Evelyn gave the wooden lance to Endell,
But against metal it did not bode well.

Heavy it was and not easily broke,
Still he feared Silas single strong stroke.
The black horse charged with rider and lance,
Giving Endell on foot only one chance.
Endell stood in a crouch, in path of spear,
Watching the poisonous black breath of Fear.
Closer it came, fast, and then closer still,
Then he dove across Fear's path with all his will.
He held the wood lance so the horse would trip,
Sending horse and rider into a flying flip.

Endell watched the pair crash and lay dazed,
He held aloft wooden lance, amazed.
        "Such strength should not exist in simple wood,
        'Tis magic of faith, defense, or intentions good,
        Though I know not, so I might be failed,
        At any moment by such power veiled.
        Still against an overwhelming will,
        Triumph; thus I name you Endurendil.
        And you can sustain me through darkest fight,
        For your virtue and vigor sides with right."

Silas struggled to rise from flying fall,
And drew his sword as his voice did call,
    "Aye, no farm do thy tend by light of day,
    Thou art champion disguised in gray,
    Doubtless a deposit upon my head,
    By the crown whose tax will rob in my stead.
    I fear matters must be set straight," he said,
    "And thou, my brave friend, must be killed dead."
He gathered shield and moved toward,
Endell, who had but a staff to a sword.

As Silas neared, Endell waved Garland,
To spirit Evelyn safely to near stand.
They joined Rodney at some safe distance,
While Endell readied his heavy lance.
He saw that Fear writhed with pain no more,
And would never carry evil to war.
Silas raised sword, preparing a blow,
Endell held his lance to fend off foe.
The first swing bit deep into the defense,
Endell swung and knocked Silas from sense.

He rolled and recovered his feet,
Silas swore, "Speed to victory not defeat,
Aggression with abandon is despair,
Reflex and reason will bring outcome fair."
Endell knew he had hope for a mistake,
    "A weaker man thou might defeat," he spake,
    "Or a woman, or a dwarf, no I forgot,
Young Rodney managed defense when you fought."
Silas laughed but his muscles clenched,
But Endell's sharp tongue was not quenched.

"Awkward unabashed methinks thou art,
Not style or fluid grace adorns your part,
Of this battle, while I, simple rustic,
With thou beside, appear full fantastic."
Silas swung with abandon at the slurs,
The arc of sword swing, bare visible blurs.
The defender turned each malicious
Attempt at artless murder most vicious.
Endell was witness to a wearying
Warrior, who saw victory fleeing.

Of all, most dangerous is sinking ship,
For no time can it bide for thou to slip.
Strike it must for no second time to fight,
Sail to harbor refuge, safe from its plight.
Or blitz the brave enemy to destroy,
Before destroyed by his mere employ.
The villain chose latter, to kill or be,
A final flurry brought Endell to one knee.
Rivulets red ran down arms to his head,
Much longer this fury, he would be dead.

Rodney reigned his pony with Evelyn,
Who wore a worried look, at battles din.
Others from the bridge, fearfully withdrew,
To the shadows, none would give his due.
Endell fought alone, yet as he began,
To fall with final flurry, Rodney ran,
To his cart where he searched a weapon,
Though he moved every vegetable, found none.
All the while the giant raged and rained,
Blows on Endell and misfortune he'd gained.

Endell blocked the blows without a thought,
For their speed denied the opening sought,
To throw the great green giant down and pounce.
Endurendil caused strokes to bounce,
Angering Silas to further fury,
And fueling Evelyn and Rodney's worry.
Endell's mind began to strangely wander,
Of plants and planets he began to ponder.
Of movement and mutability seen,
A docile desire for delight serene.

Thinking such thoughts and turning the blows,
Started him toward victory and woe.
Not full aware, his movements did linger,
Then fateful swing removed a finger.
No pain at first, only blood in torrents,
The lost left little digit brought back sense.
An apple momentarily adorned,
Silas' head, though he was now warned.
Rodney launched a rain of fruit upon,
The giant, who with one final swing was gone.

Endell on both knees felt arms collapse.
Evelyn screamed or young Rodney perhaps . . .
Lost blood and brave fight were taking their toll.
He knelt with a lance focused on his goal,
At Silas, sword raised to kill, he threw.
He fell full faint while Endurendil slew.
Evelyn removed him from the field,
Where injuries could be tended and healed.
The news of Silas death reached the King,
Who sent a messenger, Endell to bring.

Endell though weakened in limb was borne,
In triumph before the king who adorned,
The brave Endell with sword and shield,
That marked him as Marshall of the Field.
    "Sir, large reward, we with honor bestow,
For fighting and defeating our foe.
A chest of gold, a plot of land amends,
For he whose sword Silas could not defend.
Dear subjects we may all sleep more sound,
Knowing that Silas is in the cold ground."

    "With magnificent gifts and such honor,
Great king, I still rank not in your long lore.
I will accept what weapons and small fee,
Befit me and can help my errantry.
Yet nothing more shall I take or consume,
Save your leave to wander round and resume,
Adventures, for surely other danger,
Lurks and threaten manor houses to mangers."
"Fair said! So fair in fact I shall insist,
That you take the empty Castle Gremquest."

    "Upon your word I shall make my fortress,
At Gremquest, yet my word shall not regress.
Live there, no, not until my name leads,
Lore lists with glorious Garland my steed.
Now fair king what deviltry doth exist,
Within this land or just beyond border mist,
That I may avail interest upon?"
"Silas was the single scourge, since gone,
Only rumors and reports of evil,
If true could cause a great deal of upheaval."

"Then soon shall I wander the very border,
From whence these evils rise so to deter,
These black and four misguided souls which do,
Evil, yet know not of the horror's hue,
Nor peace of soul or of each simple day,
Something powerful has led them astray.
Still those on the narrow course of virtue,
Must be protected from the ugly spew,
Of such a bane, which seeks fair harmony.
Waste upon wreck is not an agony.

"Young Rodney might your family and you,
Take Gremquest and organize it in lieu,
Of my presence until I persevere,
And remove the foul elements of fear,
From the citizens and kingdom's bounds?
In sooth I will rest not 'til they are found.
When I return you shall remain with me,
Seneschals of Gremquest your family."
"But Sir Endell, you needst have a squire,
When you descend and dwell in danger dire."

"Such thought is true, I require an adjunct,
Yet such training has become near defunct,
So where might I find one fit and willing,
Who has faced danger and seen blood spilling?"
He lifted his eyes and looked around.
Rodney could not stay silent at such sounds,
As his mind organized the jumble,
Of thoughts, Endell began near to crumble,
With laughter, "Yes Rod, you shall be my squire,
And Evelyn will come to resolve her mire."

"What of this Gremquest this castle now mine,
Why be it empty and in sad decline?"
"Tis a castle not far from the ferry,
Where a young noble and his family,
Lived for generations until fate,
Crossed the young man's path in such state,
Of tragedy, that he was destroyed,
Before the king's wrath made nobility void.
Thus Gremquest has remained empty now,
Centuries or more by worthy king's vow."

"Justice of kings, divinely inspired,
Has God's volition, ours not required.
A lord of such a peaceful, just kingdom,
Has not one reason but rather a sum,
Of causes which point to a solution,
Which includes a fair retribution.
Is it common man's place to stand and condemn,
With no temporal authority, them
That beg forgiveness, or claim innocence?
What justice can man hope, lest he be God's prince?"

"Perhaps then it is some fanciful tale,
Embellished from some story soon stale."
"What form is the castle so forgotten?"
"Be the walls sealed and strong or rotten?
Dust will cover thick everything inside.
People have left the castle, rest to bide
Time until the king saw fit to open,
The gates, the question has been when.
The people will welcome some local knight,
To oversee affairs and minor fights."

"'Tis said by some that the fair fortress holds,
Many passageways and treasures old.
In fact the Castle Gremquest has reputation,
For magic and mythical sensation.
Ghosts of old kings advise and converse,
With lords on topics from people to purse.
Still those are old stories, probably tales,
That grow in the telling over numerous ales."
"Well gather the travelers and guests,
The first stop is Castle Gremquest."

The small party, provisioned and set,
Readied to leave Orvalee yet met,
By the king who presented a great key,
To Endell, "Castle Gremquest is thy fee,
For ridding us of Silas, terrible thief,
And thus removing to his grave our grief.
Go forth and may God guide thy judgment.
I beg tribute, a single rose be sent,
Alternative red and white will suffice.
To acknowledge me liege lord, but a small price."

"And thus it shall be great and noble king,
A fragrant rose each year shall I bring,
And hand to you before I worthy be,
Of admiration or mere company.
Your leave great king, and I sure, shall ride,
To Gremquest and leave it occupied."
The king waved forward the sturdy band,
Headed by Endell with four-fingered hand.
Through the leagues and little adventure,
They rode, speaking together without censure.

"This has been very hard on me dear one,"
Said Evelyn, he knew she spake not in fun,
For since red river incident,
On Endell she had much attention spent.
He had thought much of ferryman's plight.
Some second effect of the river blight,
Might she have, like he who must stay nearby,
The red river for daily drink, or die?
Could magic cause this configuration,
And what might start its rehabilitation?

Yet start he must, but then again, why so?
Of the grip of magic he did not know,
Nor if true, for they had shared much talk,
And time in travel as Garland walked.
Could it be no magic hath clouded her heart,
And she felt for Endell, whose fighting art,
Had sustained her through malediction,
Until a time they had the plague outrun.
He knew he had grown rather protective,
Of her, but yet had little time to give.

With the flight from the forest set aside,
They might return to Gremquest to reside,
Thought Endell, did it matter if magic,
Caused her emotion? Was that tragic?
He wanted a wife so she a blonde youth,
Beautiful with regal bearing in sooth,
Would well do and seemed full willing: nay,
Excited and elated when he did say,
     "Evelyn dear, I have felt all the while,
     We should be married soon and in style."

"You read my mind, I have long waited,
For this I feel in my heart was fated.
'Twas marked magic the moment we met,
Yet we've much to do before all is set.
My curse must be removed forever,
Ere we have magic and mayhem together.
One in pursuit as we pursue peace,
For this kingdom to purchase, not to lease.
The price of a life or many, is better,
Than the trickle of hope unfettered."

"These problems may have single remedy,
Silas was this land's only enemy,
For years, yet once we came reports abound,
Of evil on the borders all around.
'Tis my guess your curse has followed near,
And gathered strength, surrounding us here,
In this kingdom carved from yon forest.
For fulfilling their deed they are obsessed,
To save this space we must draw away
Attention, for all will perish if we stay."

"Rod, which direction shows the open air?"
"Open air? You mean the wood ends somewhere?
Garadreium is magic incarnate,
The Faery Queen herself in nature's state.
We know of no end or edge of wood,
Save some civic enclaves which have stood,
Against the tide of trees on all sides,
So none of us could serve as guides."
"Then follow the trails with trust in fate,
Hope even as evil lies in wait."

As Gremquest neared, Endell spoke to all
The company, "The Castle black and tall,
Must be reclaimed from time and elements.
This charge I leave 'til I return from whence,
The defense of this kingdom takes me.
And Rodney's father, Ward, Seneschal be,
Forever and for now, and yet I know,
Of the task before you, yet not below,
Though I be lord the challenge is yours,
Success, nay, fair fight opens doors."

The company departed leaving three,
On the road to consider the trees.
They plunged into the wild wood headlong,
Yet soft and silent their footfalls gone.
Past oak and beech, past bush and flower,
Through brambles and roots, minutes into hours.
They had no path, nor rough road to follow,
Progress seemed short and all hope hollow.
Yet struggle did they, their path to prove,
To find one straight and narrow but smooth.

Black breath on all sides, a wide ocean,
Of evil intent, washed past their motion.
Close, so near the tension snapped with scream,
Evelyn begged her torment, "Stop this dream!"
She reigned her steed and looked wildly,
At the woods for a moment, then mildly,
    "Take me! The curse has won, though free I was,
    For a little while. Love, credit your cause,
    For with such victory you shall be great.
    Demons arrive soon to deal out my fate."

Rod and his mount stared with wide eyes,
At Evelyn, but Endell had surmised,
Evil had entered her visual
Experience incarnate in a duel,
With the thoughts of hopelessness in escape.
She could see the very jaws of Hell agape.
He reared Garland and leapt toward her,
Endell took the reins and Garland spurred.
They emerged from the envelope of night,
Back in light, was Evelyn to Rodney's sight.

"Never give in to anything evil,
Pay no heed beyond escape, save to kill,
A malignant parasite which feeds,
On the honesty that charity bleeds.
We have hope in abundance and a will,
That drives our bodies with goals to fulfill.
Evelyn, we shall see the wide open sky,
Together, or I, in the attempt, will die."
Brush growth broke, a road crossed their path,
A chance in the race with the curse's wrath.

The way was graded smooth and fair, to hoof,
Or cart, yet remained to eye aloof,
For turn it did so often and again,
Avoiding rock and tree, that one might pain,
And grow tense not being able to see.
"Follow on, no rest or wait to weary.
Each turn I beg to find some evil stand,
So the strain of flight is in our hands."
"Fear, I have not for myself, but for love,
Which will perish, save, by gift from above."

Round the next corner they found another,
But despair not did they, nay, yet rather,
Laugh at the path uncertain as they.
Round the bend in revelry, then full stay,
Of movement, the highway splendidly straight.
A direct flight to their ultimate fate.
They broke into full career, though no end,
Seen, the road seemed to forever extend.
A glimpse of salvation appeared,
Before they were blocked by what they feared.

Without slowing Endell held his right hand,
In front of him like a ward to the band.
He brandished Endurendil as well,
In effort to defend from the horror, fell.
Giants crouched to receive the three,
Who charged and made no attempt to flee.
Other creatures held the forest flank,
Bodies covered in black slime that stank.
The black breath coated thick the very air,
Endurendil glowed with a golden glare.

Vengeful was its light, yet horror stood,
Fast came the company knowing they could,
Break the bar that threatened advance,
With trust in fate and sturdy golden lance.
At the moment of contact evil fell,
But one giant swung through Endurendil,
Slashing Rodney's pony from under him,
And creating a scene rather grim.
The pony stood, for a moment, shocked,
By the blow and then began a slow walk.

Soon a line of blood showed the extent,
Of the swing, and with a step the flesh rent,
Wide, from neck to back flank, and gushed blood,
And the pony knelt in the full red flood,
And gave Rodney, who was thrown circus clear,
A doleful look and a single true tear,
Before dying in virtue, evil near,
With Rodney to bear, never knowing fear.
Rodney shed a companion tear in silence,
Then saw a panorama immense.

A wide grassland prairie greeted his gaze,
He knocked his head because of the daze,
From his fall, then a hand on his shoulder,
And Rodney spun to see Endell's laughter.
    "The evil projected an endless run,
    To enhance the hopelessness we tried to shun.
    Once past we broke the spell, and the forest eves,
    Were upon us, all but the last leaves,
    We had passed unknown but to horror.
    Now curse is thrown down and gone is terror."

Evelyn pointed a shaky finger back,
At the wood whose eyes were crowding black.
Every manner of evil stood staring.
    "Be gone yon hellions, you are past caring!"
Then they all began to melt with a hiss,
And a black mist rose and was wind kissed,
Nothing remained save the memory,
Of another feat for greater glory.
Endell had defended the kingdom wide,
With only Evelyn and Rodney by his side.

"The curse is struck down and follows no more,
We can proceed with our lives. And lore
Of the kingdom shall record this true feat,
And all the king's subjects, like sheep, will bleat,
In praise of saving their mean lives,
For none aspire as do I, to dive,
To the deepest place or to climb the heights,
To breathe the mountain air and see all sights,
To roam the unknown and fight for my right,
To raise my wretched life into the light!"

"So noble your drive but not humble tone,
At least fight for common men who've sown,
Their lives in simplicity, so you,
Can rise above them, one of very few,
Who are worthy of their admiration,
Because the rabble decides the duration,
Of your reign as hero. Treat them well,
Remember, you are not immune, from hell,
And its wishes. We would be wise to trust,
In that fate which rules us dust to dust."

Canto II

Endell chanced upon a flower fair,
And he marveled at its sweet liqueur.
Petals of purest white with stem so green,
That other plants did envy such sheen.
With fragrance which compelled every soul,
To make songs its virtue to extol.
Lilies and orchids that stood all around,
Made no match of the scent of beauty bound,
In this flower known as Avowan by those,
With noble knowledge or healer's clothes.

He gently bore one from its place with earth,
Enough to renew it and give rebirth,
In some castle sanctuary secure.
For this the emblem of his lady pure,
Who cradled the gift while he softly spoke,
Of the past and future and of fair folk,
Who awaited their return to new life.
Then he knelt to ask, "Will you be my wife?"
She flung her arms about Endell's strong neck,
    "Oh yes, love, through time shall we trek."

Gremquest busily prepared for the feast,
To which all were invited largest to least.
The joy of the people was hardly less,
Than Evelyn's rapture and happiness.
The castle was covered from walls high,
To the gardens and quests all nigh,
With sweetest Avowan the flower fair,
Which replaced with joy any man's despair.
The flower graced even the banner,
Of the house with a majestic manner.

A single Avowan shown o'er a field,
Of brightest silver sheen shaped as a shield,
Which in turn lay on a wide swath of gold,
Producing a pennant beautiful to behold.
The visage broke over the once bleak castle,
And brought a smile to visitor and vassal.
Since the kingdom was delivered from threat,
From which Evelyn ran and brave Endell met,
His reputation doubled his true deeds,
But as with weeds and discord, not even the seeds.

The sun broke each new day with wonderment,
For the land's bounty seemed heaven sent.
Years passed in peace, with rain and winter warm,
Yet this idyllic life was broken by storm.
Out of the north it raged and frothed white,
Snow poured like cream from the sky all night.
Wind screamed a million demon's names,
While ice spirits played destructive games.
The rising sun broke none of the mad fury,
And snow still fell with wild winds of worry.

Endell rose to the silent, soft white fields,
For farms could provide only battle shields.
Defense against so sudden an onslaught,
Was not possible even had men fought,
A much weaker force than the earth they knew,
And its agents, or so they thought to be true.
Endell called his high seneschal to speak,
On which course of action they should seek,
For Endell was suspicious of this campaign,
These legions of winter caused by summer's wane.

Endell turned as a tall knight approached,
Strong he was of limb and soul, neither broached.
Though tests enough had both at the lists,
Stalwart and loyal to his lord, with no mist,
To obscure his true purpose or give disguise,
No screen of deception or handful of lies,
Did this knight possess or have muster to feed,
For this man was Rodney, once child in need.
Few years change a full man but only a shade,
Yet years for the young, and youth will quickly fade.

Time makes one half of a man the other brave deeds,
For a child can be man if he bravery breeds,
And many an old man hath never stood ground,
And faced his fears and enemy down.
Rodney came to take council, to decide a path,
Which Endell might lead or follow with wrath.
> "This foul blanket," Endell exclaimed, "must go!
> I fear dire evil blackness caused this snow.
> Yet what or who I do not know, save only,
> That I will ride faithful Garland, even lonely."

And Rod replied, "Two things are amiss with that;
I shall go with you regardless of what,
You search, even if I crawl behind your trail,
And also, what objective will this quest assail?
A quest has a definite goal at end,
Or we become knights errant, virtue to defend."
    "Too true dear Rodney, my spirit again soared.
    Faith, we need an objective to move toward."
    "If one is looking for evil and has no fear,
    Perhaps an oracle gaze at the Mithomere?"

    "Splendid my boy, we ride into the dawn,
    So prepare my dukedom and my horse, be gone,
    I ride true Garland my steed back to the wood,
    Garadreium is fearsome but there I have stood,
    And faced true threat and terror twenty fold,
    That of mere wind and weather and biting cold.
    I must tell Evelyn of this trip," he thought.
He gave a signal a silent servant sought,
    "Find the duchess and fetch her to me. Be quick,
    I've much to do 'fore dawn lights morning's wick."

    "My love, dearest Evelyn, be not distraught,
    At my wandering, for answers are sought,
    To this attack, this outrage against our land.
    We must gather courage and take a stand."
    "I understand, you must leave for a time,
    To crush what evil has changed our clime.
    Yet fear I shall, for you 'til you return,
    To me whole and alive with Garland stern."
She placed a chain around Endell's neck,
    "Take this token, a pendant, on your trek."

Endell kissed her brow and swept her hair back,
He smiled softly his love shone without lack.
　　"Fear, I have none, save for you my dearest,
　　Especially with this danger queerest."
He looked down to the pendant and saw,
An enameled Avowan without flaw,
He laughed, "Such is doubtless the best cure,
For solemn times and speeches 'tis sure.
I may be long away upon the quest,
For until I slay the bane I shall not rest!"

The day dawned fair with fearful cold.
Endell and Rodney astride their mounts bold,
Issued from Gremquest gate with a squire or two,
Rodney's mount Vega, white with a darker hue,
A mere suggestion around its strong head.
The group faced the crowd and Endell said,
　　"Fear not, as I. Faith be not fallen now,
　　Nor if I return with blood upon my brow."
He turned his steed in silence slow,
Walking from Gremquest is search of the foe.

Some days and knights had passed their path,
Through the fallen snow whose weakening wrath,
They noticed the further on they went.
Each step the snow more shallow with intent.
They soon found shelter in the forest great,
Which full made the kingdom an island state,
In the magic of Garadreium Wood,
For the forest shelters little that is good.
Shadows harbor those who seek to hide,
Or remain beyond approach, time to bide.

The white cover held its ground until,
The travelers came to the forest still.
No snow nor sound of bird or beast was there,
Yet the air was warm with sunlight to spare.
  "Where the beasts?" said Endell, "And birdsong bright?
  What evil force has them in flight?"
  "'Twas fear of the cold," said a quiet voice,
  "Half were unprepared and had no choice.
  The better half, just that, they fled for love,
  From the largest bear to the turtledove."

The voice was all around. They held hard fast,
And looked for a man and movement vast,
Or minute enough to suggest some life
Was attached to this true tale of strife.
Silence greeted each glance until again,
  "They've gone I say, far away from pain."
  "Who art thou that speaks and even now remains
  Alone, so alone that you by proxy reigns?"
  "Oh, no king am I, though not without skill,
  In arts of science I can command my will."

The voice came small and less omnipotent,
From near the setting sun it came impotent
Of all the power and splendor which held
The company to mystery compelled.
Then near a tree in the face of the sun,
Stood a stooped old man, a ragged one.
  "Come," he waved, "these trees I know. Follow."
He ambled toward a hill and hollow.
He walked straight to the sun though no path
Could be seen before him. He left a wide swath.

"I wonder who this wanderer is my lord,"
Queried Rodney beneath his breath and sword.
"There be some strong magic in that old man,
We should go wary as cautious as can."
"Fear not this wizard," commanded Endell,
"Party to counsel not subject to spell
Are we by this many hued magician
Whose advice will be a welcome addition."
They passed the trees to a sheltered dell,
Where a mound held a door made of seashell.

A low fire burnt so shadows leapt up each wall,
Like an animal reaching for food or a ball.
Like a man trying to touch heaven high,
Time and again without knowing why.
The room strange shaped, stuffed with books and herb,
And dust so thick that movement could not disturb.
A silence brewed, many stout lost years,
Guarded like the very secret of all fears.
A corner held a small suit of armor,
Dull, so eyes passed, nothing to deter.

Many crags held various interests to light,
Though the single torch, near the fire to the right.
On the walls a faint pattern played fire,
And conceived a network of desire.
Attention full riveted to the dance,
Even at the slightest chance passing glance.
"Sit my friends," smiled the host who did,
"Rest your legs and of your pains be rid.
We have time to talk, indeed I will tell,
Of horror and humor and evil fell."

Endell was now intent upon the little man,
But Rodney shifted his glance like windblown sand.
The fire flickered forth in the silence,
Raising light and shadow to high violence.
>"Came the cold," intoned the man as the fire fell,
>"A cold even my magic could not quell.
> I found not the nature of this peril,
> Only that it connects to a King Arrol."
Endell blinked, that name he had heard before,
Long ago in some forgotten tale of lore.

The flames in the short silence slowly rose,
>"Is that person known by you whose face froze?"
The fire became but a mere glow of embers,
>"Is there anything that anyone remembers?"
With a will not entirely his own Endell
Related his knowing; he had heard the name fell.
>"How was this man brought forth and involved,
> And what might he play in the crime solved?"
>"If we find this King then we might know all,
> But this means we should not waste time and stall."

>"We strike for the Mithomere," Rodney spake,
>"In fact we travel for this very sake.
> Cold far worse grips yonder farms in evil charms,
> And many people will not weather these harms."
>"You are rash, young Rod, though that not strange,
> Yet if you wish long life this too must change."
He held up his hand to hold the hail and howl,
>"I beg you leave to pursue this evil foul."
Endell thought out loud, "A wizard with us,"
He straightened slow, "Yes it should be thus."

"And no mere magician am I," quoth he,
"I command the wind and converse with tree.
Best still a secret path to Mithomere
I can guide you through with but little queer,
For like all forest ways it is never clear
Completely of calamity or tear.
We shall go to the oracle water,
To search for purity's nymph daughter,
Who will reveal some reality to light,
This darkness which envelops earth and plight."

Those few preparations which wizards make,
Were made and soon they left for speeds' sake.
The wizard led and told at length fair tales,
Of princes play, knightly pranks, and quiet vales.
Though he tried, this ancient man concealed,
Nothing of his past yet little more revealed.
He knew a man, Sebastian, of whom he spoke,
So well that all began to suspect a joke,
But before once voice was heard the old man said,
        "The name is Herorot that rests upon my head."

"My father, 'tis said, was traveling that road,
Which runs from sea to capital, King's abode.
The Anchor and Crown, an inn he soon neared,
And warnings he heard yet none that he feared,
Of a beast, dragon like though wingless, and fierce,
With hide so hideous strong no point could pierce.
This worm had taken the inn and many full men,
Who had stood their ground both since and when,
The worm came and claimed land and beer alike,
From the inn and also any who dared to strike.

"But my father was a fighting man from birth
And cared little for fair words save in mirth.
He took a stiff swig of liquor, wiped his lip,
Then armed with sword and shield, took another sip.
He sallied into the inn, silence in command,
And faced the horrific bulk sword in hand.
No sound came for much time and people grew chill,
Nameless death had visited again to kill,
Tension grew, and grew 'til my father came forth,
A large mug of mead merged with his mouth.

" 'Enter', he cheered, the beast is dead though how
I know not, only that I struck no blow'.
They drank into the night though my father left
Quietly the town and me with my mother bereft.
She gave me, my name, and the story away
To a childless couple who were old and gray.
Kind they were yet dead before a score of years.
My sorrow shed the first and last of my tears."
"But what of this Sebastian?" queried Rod,
"Is he fact or simply a fictitious fraud?"

A faraway look glazed Herorot's eyes,
Reflecting a soul where emotions revise,
And examine again each facet in time,
Of a relationship, to seek out some crime,
Or blame in a matter not yet undone.
Then he slowly said, "He was my only son."
He stared, then shook his eyes with purpose,
          "But that was long ago and farther than thus."
He waved his hand toward the mountain stand,
Seeming to brush away memory like smoke fanned.

The others of the fellowship remained,
Silent and from further questions refrained.
Soon the subject fell from each of their thoughts,
All save the seer, the magician Herorot.
The land now loomed over this band of men,
The mountains were in the majority when,
Each eye was lifted, the horizon to scan.
One wondered where peak ended and sky began.
The land rose, yet a valley they followed,
To the mountain root then they were swallowed.

The entrance a cave with darkness oozing,
Malevolent with lack of light diffusing,
Into the wood a groping evil hand,
Reaching, reaching like a tide on the strand.
Remnants only of a door once ornate,
Framed the yawning blackness giving weight
To nameless fears which well in every breast,
When the heart is by the ribs caressed.
Breath is short, the nerves tingle and time true,
Seems to multiply its span giving wider view.

"Follow fearless," spake Herorot with calm control,
Though no one knew he spoke with hyperbole.
He found a phial inside his great cloak of magic,
A jewel, an element of light fantastic.
He held it aloft and blackness broke revealing,
No cave but a wide grassy plain with no ceiling.
"What deviltry is this?" cried Endell for he feared,
His hand clutching to his brooch and all disappeared.
A scream broke his thought and he spun to see,
The wall being smote by a sword held by Rodney.

Again with a triumphal shout sword bit stone,
For there was no enemy save to Rodney alone.
Yet not, some evil did dwell in delusion,
For false was this fantasy, an illusion.
A wide plain to one, moving stone to another.
Even each squire stood with wide face asunder.
Confusion with each episode before his eyes,
Wondering if evil or each single mind lies.
Perceptions danced as the party remained,
Rooted unable to escape though unchained.

   "Begin we must," spoke Endell slow without fears,
   "The great grassland is very wide it appears."
   "Best we keep ahead," agreed Herorot unsure,
Of Endell's motivation his own sight a blur.
   "Away," cried Endell's squire as he leapt high,
And plunged the ground with his dagger, dry,
To all eyes save his, for black blood soaked his blade,
And a tentacle twitched in death in Endell's shade.
But he had gone perceiving not the danger,
Nor heroism by his attendant stranger.

Rod too had turned to follow his lord,
Down the dark passage from stone full scored.
He marveled at mighty Endell fearless,
And saw his life with uncommon clearness,
Though only for a moment, then veil fell,
Into its customary place again pell-mell.
Like other instants of illumination,
There was no clue to the coming sensation,
And the mind a moment past cannot grasp,
That elusive element of perception past.

Though each mind encountered endless enigma,
To all others, each did not perceive a flaw.
Each man acted on his own concept of all,
But do not all men follow this course who crawl,
Or walk or run in any direct action?
Is then reality not a full function,
Of each man's perception, be then sane or no?
For even insane can have their effect show.
The gathering of individual perception,
Is in truth reality without exception.

Now as they moved and each his thought merged,
The confusion at the first fell submerged,
By equal experience in exertion to task,
And an excitement that danger could not mask.
A forest now faced the five full dark,
Each step echoed the last, lonely, deep, stark.
No sunlight saw this forest floor for not one
Flower, colored the drab ground devoid of sun.
Rotting wood and dead leaves formed a great pall,
Which covered the land like the blight of sprawl.

Into the endless seeming drear Endell strode,
        "Near to the end are we Herorot, I bode."
        "What end though I wonder," replied the old man,
As a shout of voices broke the silent land.
Quickly Endell sprang toward the empty fight,
Rodney followed, yet not with the magicians might.
For the old man melted into the scene swift,
And found a vantage from which he could drift,
If the fight turned to flight for his friends,
Yet still he hoped his magic would make amends.

Endell burst into the glade his sword in shade,
To Endurendil his mythic lance he bade,
      "Go well, true staff and see me through this day.
      Come Rod, for truth we must enter the fray.
      My guess has the multitude miscreant,
      And that lone warrior on guard defiant.
      To fight! Sweet Endurendil yet preserve us!"
With that he loosed himself upon the evil thus;
A sweep of his shaft and two of the twelve fell,
They moved not, either, for their eyes remained of hell.

All seeing are those of Hades yet nothing seen,
Save evil all around and every deed that's been.
No future joy, no love, only jealous rage,
Tormented by sight unriven even by age.
Those souls have fixed the ghastly light of hell,
In their always open eyes, evil's spell.
The two dead by Endell's blow, stared red,
Their eyes with the devil's fury in his stead.
Still ten wraiths of men remained,
And now their wrath on Endell they reigned.

As if renewed by help yon warrior struck.
A weighted chain whistled the wind, though luck
Had no part in its passion or pain,
For heavy metal links left five wraiths slain.
Their dull eyes soon glowed as coals of hell,
Flickering ghastly red, an evil well.
Now seven gone yet five remain riven,
For evil and fear thrives the more given.
Thus these five turned and fled with fear dead,
      "We will return to strike again!" they said.

The warrior dropped his chain in pain,
His hand burnt where link on palm had lain.
　　"My hand has never dealt such devastation,"
Said he, as he held it to soothing sensation,
And he looked down to see white smoke rise,
As the chain withered gone to winds disguise.
　　"Well, Sir Warrior, who mayst thou be?"
Asked a jovial Endell, formally.
　　"Kevin, is me, protector of . . ." he turned,
　　But she was gone, . . . "one who isn't concerned."

　　"There is a girl I swear and did my love,
　　Though for pure proof I gave my gauntlet glove."
He held his hand high, no armor was there,
And to Endell's amaze his sword hand was bare.
　　"This princess she bears the prize to her father,
　　I must guard her and it, if I want her.
　　She goes fast to make my task difficult,
　　This task of errantry more than barely felt.
　　Still that chain and five wraiths are here no more,
　　And I survive to fight again my war."

　　"Twas me, twas me!" sang Herorot from above,
　　"I charged the chain with power beyond love."
　　"Beyond love?" spake Endell, "Such power exists?"
　　"Indeed, indeed," nodded magician though mists,
Clouded his eyes and his voice trailed unsure,
　　"Perhaps 'twas my love and care which I infer,
　　A purer love resting upon true friendship,
　　Rather than the physical desire which trips
　　Many into a false belief of love deep,
　　And always encourages someone to weep."

" 'Twas me who charged the chain with white heat,
Enough I judge to cripple Mephisto's treat."
"Join us Sir Knight so we might help each other,
Your name and pledge are all we need dear brother."
"Kevin," he said without pause, "and I engage
Myself as knight in fellowship without wage.
And you brave knight now undertake for your house."
And Endell bowed low, "From Evelyn my spouse,"
Said he with the sweep of his hand, "And all here,
To mad maids newborn son or empty mug 'o beer.

"My troth is pledged, an oath I swear to thee,
I'll save your life and find your wife for free."
Endell smiled and lo a grin broke,
And he laughed so loud the glade awoke,
And every which way ran nature's progeny,
Hither and thither though heather and weather.
Beasts ran birds flew from the laughter like a storm,
All manner of life even insect swarm.
Yet none took notice of the completeness,
Of the event to which they had been witness.

"Well wizard," Endell asked, "What of the girl?
This oath and our quest make something of a whirl."
"Indeed but counsel I must to Mithomere,
For 'tis, I'm sure, very close to here,"
And as Kevin rose to protest he waved,
"Quiet! Come, I can hear the fountain; twice knave!"
They pushed through the wood and lo came the sound,
Falling water and the noise of all drops drowned.
For the splash more a gasp of ecstasy,
Tempered with a hint of hesitancy.

"Mithomere," murmured Rodney, "And so near."
"How? Our wizard reckoned nothing save by ear."
"We have traveled little," Herorot said,
"Tis true, o'er land and through wood from dread to dread,
We can reckon our travel space though not,
In time, hark to the magical wood lot,
Which we entered with its wild distortion,
Removing from all minds a sense of proportion.
And here we are, our goal, forget not your fear."
He motioned them look, "Mind this Mithomere!"

Arrived they had for now the true splendor,
Met their eyes and each moment did engender,
Their souls with wonder and truth beyond measure,
For each thought now transformed to a treasure.
More value than gold or gemstone or trifle,
Touched with holiness each moment did not stifle,
The projection of reality beyond the now,
Into the boundless void your mind might allow.
Though a weak mind has not power to direct,
An oracle can oft respond to respect.

A fountain's pool, the mere which might reflect,
The future of past on some truth you inspect.
Each drop fell into the pool though no ripple,
Stained the surface though violence did triple,
With the thrice higher pulse of the fountain's height
The mere remained calm, the company contrite.
Once natural, this pool, and obvious still,
Though a golden rail offered safety from spill.
        "Touch not the mere say all accounts and lore,
        For each drop has magic beyond peace and war.

"Away, away from the mere's edge say I,
      Much must be marshaled 'fore this marvel we try!"
Suddenly solemn the company saw with scope,
How the magic might leave them without mere hope.
Though how small a thought is hope when compared
To emotions, 'tis the thing that first comes bared,
Never lost, even in despair always there,
Yet alone betrayed by action unfair,
For hope never exists where a thing cannot,
Yet with slightest chance hope is always sought.

"You all watch me and wait so in your turn,
      The secrets of the Mithomere you will learn.
      Each has one answer ready, every man,
      Comes to seek clues to what question he can."
Herorot moved to the mere as a magnet,
Might attract a forgotten metal fragment,
His gaze fixed beyond the watery surface,
Though he alone knew his personal purpose.
None could see even a ripple in the pool,
Yet something whole held Herorot in deepest duel.

The ecstasy he endeavored to hold,
Twisted his form, and he writhed with sweat sold,
By bold imagination and brief suggestion,
Taken where it was not his true intention.
Joy to horror, voiceless fear and wild eyes
Showed the company how delight dies.
Herorot, despite his dread had his orbs held
To the same spot steadfast and mental weld.
From his knees he rose to scream his only word,
And he fell again crumpled, his senses blurred.

No one moved to Herorot's dusty form,
Silence proceeded the coming storm.
A trickle of blood started from his ear,
And every man said something tinged with fear.
The one word epitaph of ecstasy heard,
From Herorot's horror which death had cured.
    "Guilty!" he had screamed and moaned with a word,
Through his throes of horror his companions stirred.
What now, who next the mere? Though all knew.
To the last man Endell endured their view.

Endell the fearless felt eyes on his face,
His flesh burned with fear but there was no trace.
His heartbeat he was sure was heard by each,
So he leapt to fill the silence and beseech,
Those with faint fortune to stand not in fear,
While he convinced himself to Mithomere.
    "I see brave knights, a magician's folly,
    I see courage raped, hearts once jolly,
    Now fearful and eyes unable to meet
    Any foe unless they witness routed retreat."

He brandished his sword and smote the air,
    "To arms! For all that is sacred and fair.
    Remember the pestilence which struck
    Our farms, our homes, running amok.
    I shall stay and gaze into this oracle,
    For I shan't allow this quest to debacle!"
He started to the mere though silence reigned
His cause not taken up, his men restrained.
    "Stop," a voice quietly spoke, then again,
    "Stop!" Endell slowly turned to face the refrain.

One knight stood now, his true stature revealed.
He advanced upon Endell and kneeled.
        "Lord, I must do this deed and I shall swear,
        Upon the very veil of Mithomere there.
        In this role I am cast I have felt it.
        I protect my lord, as I must, it is writ."
And Endell looked long into heaven,
Then smiled into those eyes of Kevin,
        "Everyman will sample the oracle who can,
        I am here for my people and their land."

And Kevin strode stiffly toward the mere,
Casting aside his armor, sword and spear,
For those would help not in a contest which
Pitted his convictions against a switch
Of his will under the pressure of magic.
He steeled his thoughts from the tragic,
He stopped at the rail with eyes to heaven
And counted aloud until reaching seven,
Then with all eyes upon him he knelt,
And reached for water until he felt.

With touch, a silence crept through Kevin's mind,
Like meandering thought consciousness can find.
The trees and grass now revealed a voice,
And fully laid bare, was his future and choice.
The folly of his betrothed was clear,
A woman, who wants security from fear,
Had put them both at risk by baring his hand.
'Twas foolish to let the request stand,
Surely the deep wood was tortuously tough,
Even together and armed enough.

Convince her, your concern for security,
Spoke the pool with a ripple of purity.
For women want safety above all else,
Once given any chill, a female heart melts.
And for Kevin the reverie was done.
His hand no longer in touch, and spell none.
He smiled. At first so wide that others gasped,
Like he was in some unnatural state clasped,
He spoke, "The mere, 'tis wise and still to fear,
But I am through and my own path is clear."

     "I must leave, Lord Endell, but return I shall.
     For my path is sure to Castle Doral.
     Where I wed my princess Laurel most fair,
     And return to you with a lock of her hair,
     As proof to my quest and faith in enterprise,
     Which you thus engage yourself without disguise."
And Endell smiled and said, "Harm not a hair,
Of Laurel's wreath, it might draw unwanted stares.
Your faith I am full sure will prove out true,
When you return. So off to Laurel and your due."

Now Endell's smile flew and his task true at hand,
He knelt at the rail, to crystallize his thought bland,
Of the future, his concern directed,
Yet his mind with the oracle not connected.
Endell hoped for guidance to remove snow,
And return the little kingdom from woe.
His hand shook as he slowly reached down.
His charges watched wide-eyed his renown.
Just inches above the Mithomere glass,
Endell's four fingered hand held fast.

The bottomless pool glowed faint yellow light,
Under his hand gathering together bright.
Endell's eyes went wide though body fixed,
His hope and his horror helplessly mixed.
The bright watery spot bubbled and boiled,
But Endell's hand remained uncoiled.
Then a hand emerged from the oracle's surface,
And grabbed Endell's wrist with dire purpose.
Rodney whooped and grabbed for his sword,
And as he unleashed his blow, he roared.

Endell had only moments with Mithomere,
Intimate seconds where all was clear.
With a clarity which others were denied,
Endell saw his problem and future laid wide.
Vast armies and a crown lay under his spell,
While flags fluttered, nobles gathered to quell,
A growing evil not so trivial as snow,
But something beyond that overwrought blow.
Endell saw a situation beyond grim,
Where his support was failing and hopes slim.

In the darkness before the battle's dawn,
Endell commands armies but is history's pawn.
A messenger enters – "King Arrol I bring news.
Our allies have come and would know what you choose!"
A calming smile broke on Endell's kingly face,
        "The tide is swung, we must make haste.
        Instruct them down the hill to guard retreat,
        And our strategy will be complete."
Held to the oracle Endell was rapt,
'Til at Rodney's brash sword stroke it snapped.

Rodney, fearful of the handhold bold,
Sprung forth, raised his sword, and severed hold.
He sliced just below the water line,
And freed Endell but now himself combined,
Splashed with the power of the oracle.
The water sparkling his skin like a manacle.
Rod's eyes rolled back into his head,
And he fell like a stone apparently dead.
Endell still squat by oracle's side,
Held up his bleeding hand cut wide.

No blood left the cut which ran across,
Two fingers not near to being lost.
As they gazed upon the wound they gasped.
The cut knit itself together magic clasped
The two edges healed without seam.
And the cut disappeared as in a dream.
Now Endell returned to reality,
And turned to Rodney lying in calamity.
For he moved not and his eyes wide
Shut, as someone suddenly stunned ere they died.

Endell bent to close his squire's orbs,
And tried again before he absorbed,
That Rodney yet lived though seemingly gone,
It was Mithomere's grasp that held him yon.
Endell ordered his men to bear Rod,
Away from the place where they had been awed,
By the oracle's behest. Endell knew,
That all would come well because of this view,
Of the future – where Rodney would bring,
Armies, and Endell would be King.

So back to their little kingdom to go,
Now evidence pointed to no fear of snow.
Mithomere had given courage to Endell,
Because he thought all would be well
While blind. Though still he must make it so.
For he had not seen how to deliver the blow.
Mithomere had worked its mythic magic,
Altering Endell's perception the trick,
For reality exists only as total sum,
Of everyone's belief of what was, is, and will come.

As the drops of oracle water dried
Rodney came back to waking and cried,
      "I've seen – I've seen our lands free of snow.
      The menace of cold removed by Endell's blow."
The men cheered as they made haste for home,
Eager to finish with magician, troll and snow.
      "And there's more – too horrible to speak,"
      Said Rod, "For if true the future is bleak."
      "What of it," laughed Endell. "What did you see?
      Of your death perhaps," then quietly, "Or was it me?"

But Rod remained silent as stone,
As Endell watched him and moaned.
Quickly recovering he said, "But Rod, I will die.
Was there indication of the when, where or why?"
Then Rod brightened a bit and said,
      "No lord, no time but on your head,
      You wear a crown with Avowan inlaid,
      And old with care and armed with blade.
      It seems a death heroic for no despair,
      Follows our symbol Avowan, flower fair."

Endell secretly pleased with the foretelling,
For it seemed his power and prestige were swelling,
And would reach a zenith of such renown,
That he, Endell, would be invested with the crown.
  "The spell of snow is cast down," said Endell.
  "Wither by my exercise over the well,
  Of Mithomere, or by our clashes
  On this road with several evil flashes
  Which we soundly smote and threw down,
  Perhaps Herorot was evil's clown?"

The ragged party moved through the wood,
Concerned not of their path as they should.
Mere distance their goal and their desire,
For direction they considered around the campfire.
  "We will arrive in familiar lands soon,
  As we have fulfilled our destiny's boon,"
Said Endell with certainty born of foreknowledge,
Despite there being no direction through foliage.
The campfire they tended for its light,
Certain of far future but not the night.

As sunshine filtered through forest trees,
The ragged band moved with the breeze,
Its warming lilt lent credence to Endell's tale,
That the little kingdom was no longer assailed.
And just as the telling, the tale was true.
For the group halted to rest and review.
Endell climbed a nearby crest to scout,
He gazed east seeing autumn fields all about.
Time had but fooled them and marched along,
Months passed, though only seemed days long.

With a whoop Endell ran down the slope,
And mustered his men with a view of hope.
Quickly they broke through the wood to see
Their fields and farms rendered free
Of the snow and cold and standing with corn,
And ripe with things from the earth born.
They praised Endell who delivered the land,
As locals began to gather round the band.
As they marched along towards the King,
They were cheered and feted and so began to sing.

"O'er lands known to deeds renown,
Forward, forward, we never look down.
Through tended fields under clear bright skies,
Forward, forward, until we die.
One victory complete, one champion declared,
Until we die, we will be spared.
So fight for victory, to fight again,
To fight as long as our enemies remain.
We won the fight, we battled long,
And we return scarred, wiser and strong!"

A mighty following trailed the men well,
And word of their coming rang like a bell.
Endell led as they rode toward Gremquest,
Stopping often at invitation to rest.
People rejoiced as the band approached,
Eager to thank them and offer a toast,
"To the heroes of Gremquest, each and all,
Who faced danger to remove winter's pall."
And Endell smiled at the tributes,
Proud of his doings and of his recruits.

As they approached fair Gremquest Castle,
A horseman thundered, a king's vassal.
He reigned his dusty mount in their midst.
    "Endell, I am a Messenger Royal,"
    He said with steely countenance, "Loyal,
    To the crown, sent to deliver these words. . ."
    "Hail Endell, our thanks and our faith reward,
    At leisure, point yourself and horse toward,
    Our table for time has come to bestow,
    The title 'Duke' – for defeating our foe."

The king's messenger shared Endell's grin,
And company around rose voices to a din.
    "Thank you knight," yelled Endell above the cheers,
    "Tell the King of my most humble fears.
    Yet I will accept his judgment of me,
    After Gremquest I'll join him at his decree!"
The knight nodded and thundered away,
But the company cheered their effect display.
    "To Gremquest with haste!" triumphed Endell,
    "Our winter is past and so is spell."

Garland leaped away, Rodney in pursuit,
And in their dust came the hordes, hardly mute.
And their ragged cheers caught the whistling wind,
Breeze blown to Gremquest, audible but thinned.
The quizzical sentry first noted noise,
Then gainsaid it as the expression of joys.
When dust cloud appeared did then voice take,
    "Awake, awake, to great joy Gremquest awake!
    Lord Endell returns, no more than an hour made,
    Awake, prepare for triumphal parade!"

The Castle, jolted joyous, awoke with speed,
Knowing Endell's desire and mighty steed.
Not an hour gone past when Endell came,
To a silent, spooked Castle, in game.
His brow furrowed, his wonder grew fast,
No one to meet him, at journey's long last.
As he stood pondering, Rodney made the gap,
And stood beside Endell aghast at the last lap,
A trumpet blared from the battlement wall,
And quickly the Avowan flag rose above them all.

Drawbridge dropped fast and people appeared,
Pouring forth, dotting heights and loudly cheered.
    "Hail Endell, defender of land and faith,
    You delivered us from the winter wraith."
And Endell smiled and glanced around,
Yet Evelyn was nowhere to be found.
    "I will not enter the Castle until
    I meet the King and know his will,
    Yet before I leave I will repair awhile,
    To consult with my house and share a smile."

The people made merry that day and next,
But Evelyn remained hidden and Endell was vexed.
'Til finally he asked a messenger lad,
Where was his bride, should he be sad?
    "She remains in her rooms, lord, and it's told,
    She pines though she refuses to fold.
    You left her for quest and she begs you return,
    To move first, and in this she is stern.
    At least that's the word from her maids, my lord.
    She claims sickness from the prick of a sword."

And Endell knew this truth and Evelyn more,
He rolled his eyes and smiled to implore.
    "Tell no one I've gone into Gremquest,
    My word is broken but at Evelyn's behest."
And he turned into the dark, a shade,
Creeping into the Castle his plans well laid.
He nodded at the guards of Evelyn's rooms.
They smiled, surprised, and deeply moved.
He entered her room and she asleep,
And he crept to her bed without a peep.

Endell reached to rouse her but stopped his hand,
He looked at his bride and her wedding band,
And thought how he loved her, how deeply,
And how he'd earned her love so cheaply.
Those thoughts like her tears he brushed away,
And he kissed her brow and sang this lay. . .
    "Awake when your love returns your kiss,
    He is here and now nothing's amiss.
    Awake with a smile to match my own,
    And rejoice with me, your love is come home."

Her eyes fluttered yet remained clenched,
And while Endell wondered, he guessed,
He sang again softly, now knowing her ploy.
And her smile quickly broadened showing her joy.
    "Awake, awake I'm back from my test,
    Yet I must answer our King at his behest.
He reached for her cheek, "Evelyn please,"
Then swiftly with glee her waist he did seize,
And tickled her while she begged him to cease,
Gleeful yet determined to win peace.

"Meet me astride your mount on the morrow,
And we'll ride to our King without sorrow.
We'll share the joy as Duke and Duchess,
Though I must say I expected no less."
As dawn melted mist, Evelyn rode down,
From Gremquest, silent without herald or sound.
As she stayed her mount, fanfare flared.
And Endell appeared, and for a second he stared.
In the sun, he remembered her beauty,
And stood stunned until he remembered his duty.

"Beautiful thou art," said he, true words failing,
"How could I have left you at King's hailing?"
He shook his head, and vowed that day,
Never to leave her side come what may.
His ambition he would shelf now forever,
And pledged to leave Evelyn behind never.
She'd be with him, for him to defend,
Safer than Gremquest, who's walls could rend,
And fall to strong foe, but Endell would ever,
Stay with his bride, no matter his endeavor.

They slowly moved o'er the pleasant green land,
Toward their King's golden hall as planned.
Only thanks barred their way through towns,
And soon they were led before the crown.
"Hail, Mark the King," shouted a helmeted guard.
And all rose as he entered, while began a bard.
"All praise our most reverend monarch high,
Yet he commands me a lay of Endell, nigh."
And the singer told of battles and fury,
And Endell standing forth full of worry.

"Endell, for your service you will expect
A dukedom, earldom or some other effect.
Yet you shall have them and more if you desire.
And more, All hail Endell the next king and sire."
While everyone silent, surprise shook everyone.
The king said, "I've adopted my heir. It is done."
The hall cracked with smiles and whoops of joy,
But Endell stood stone still shocked at the ploy.
He would be the next king, regal and strong,
But what then, where did his legend belong?

"Hail Endell, lord protector of this realm,
Now crown's heir who's deeds overwhelm,
Where fore you came Endell, is not known,
But you've established our trust along with renown.
Return to Gremquest yet come to us often.
You've much to know before my reign's end."
After much speech and feasting for days upon days,
Endell and Evelyn travelled to Gremquest without delays.
For their vassals must have the news known,
That Endell, their lord, was destined for throne.

As they neared the castle a mob approached,
Yet with grins and joy soon broached,
Their knowledge of events and Endell's fortune.
The pleasure of it caused Evelyn to swoon,
"Oh, the joy of it all, how happy I am,"
Said she upon reviving by a little dram.
The crowds swelled to the castle, festooned
With an array of Avowan like highest June.
Balloons, flowing food and drink, music for kings,
Nothing was forgotten, not the slightest of things.

Endell, duke of Gremquest, Earl of Avowan now called,
Titles he chose with others more involved.
Dressing in finery, first for his wife, he
Began to enjoy the best that could be.
Sharing at first with all in his house,
Soon his accounts demanded he douse
His fine tastes, at least for public perception,
And after a while his vassals were the only exception.
Endell lived high and thought higher still,
What could he do by the reign of his will?

What could he do, what could he see,
That would give leave for his greatness to be?
He waited with ease in his newfound stance,
As king's heir, yet strove to enhance,
His place, his power, and prettied his lance,
Into a thing guilt with gold, a romance
Of jewels, fine metals, and curious words,
Endurendil, once pristine wood, now seemed absurd.
For fighting men of pure heart fight not,
With ornaments, or art works they bought.
Endell dreamed as he o'er gazed the land
That soon he'd ride to war on the back of Garland.

For four months he dreamed all in a row
He battled monsters, evil and snow.
Then from the west rose a great haze,
And thunder, earth shaking, rumbling on days.
An army whose breadth and leader unknown
Swept through the sunset toward its Gremquest home.
He sleepily smiled as his conquering horde
Returned in his dreams at behest of their lord.
But no – the untold thousands returned in defeat,
His army in flight, his minions simply bleat.

And he awoke, bathed in stinging sweet sweat,
And he knew, no dream but reality met.
If today, his plans which precarious lay
Fade and die, his life, his history are stay.
Joining for battle, his smile to engender
Courage to his changes enough to remember
Through battle for glory, his deeds to relive
Yet his heart heavy his courage a sieve.
Once Endell, so long ago, now Arrol king
A name prophesied by Evelyn's ring.

He girt his armor, light yet strong,
First with foreboding, later with song.
He fastened his Avowan crown,
And fixed his sash of rank around
A trumpet blared off to his right
And horses and men clattered to fight.
He bowed his head, ready to make peace,
For his foibles, his wrongs not the least.
However came a knight, young and in love,
With battle, a lady, but with no glove.

> "Hail Arrol king, rest easy, your fame assured,
> We fight for our story to be deferred,
> King Arrol I am honored to battle today,
> The 13th time in your service, I've entered a fray.
> Victorious we will be, now I've a plan
> A dell, bowl shaped, there we will stand,
> Draw them in, and descend down to do battle
> And slay them, eat them, herd them like cattle.
> The army it moves, victory today, come now,
> Follow me to the battle, follow me to the brow."

"I lead," screamed Arrol, spurring ahead,
"I lead, I've always led, I reign till dead."
And he pushed past and into the dell,
Charged down the slope and into a battle hell.
Slicing past soldiers like snowflakes,
He slashed, thrust, battles without breaks
Toward the battle flag of the enemy host,
Spurred on by his destiny, his quiet boast,
Like a dream or a ghost to the banner,
Untouched, unbowed, in a magical manner.

Facing Arrol a king of quiet clear sight,
Who seemed somehow magic, purer of light.
Nothing said, nothing done, yet Arrol knew,
Something momentous was his due.
The other king familiar, but Arrol knew not,
Who he was, why they stood there, why they fought.
And the other king drew his sword, Arrol unmoved,
Frozen in destiny his future proved.
Blade glinted, truth flashed, his destiny just,
Light flashed, his memories faded like dust.

Canto III

Won or lost, lose or win, King Arrol lay,
Upon a swath of grass not far from fray.
Naked he, in no armor now clad,
Save what honor and true virtue he had,
Developed in his mortal life when,
He was given the chance which all men,
Are charged with when they wake to the world.
Battle remained though banner unfurled.
No trumpets sound to call forth the hosts,
No one to watch, excepting the ghosts.

No sound did echo when he lay soul still,
The air was clean yet heavy with some will,
Far greater than any shiny noble luster,
Or army some powerful king could muster.
No vault of sky hung high above his head,
Though low light existed in the sun's stead.
Horizon not, for all around a bowl,
Ringed with mountains like a shallow hole.
Streams and rivers and even wood stand,
Lay about, scattered across the land.

"The battle must have swept by since I fell,
But what of this large, vast empty dell.
I remember no such place at all,
Far from bitter battle large or small.
Was I carried away and left to rot,
In some unwholesome unknown evil spot,
Which befits not the name of a beggar,
Let alone a noble king with heart pure?
Or hath some other fate befallen me?
I beg God allow my eyes to see."

Yet the landscape remained unchanged,
Though to Arrol's sight all stayed strange.
Such a battle, what majestic splendor,
Yet with such fight what outcome rendered,
From the clash at dusk with pennants display,
With the armies both in noble array,
To the final fight of kings alone,
        "But outcome I cannot recall, unknown,
To me, even many details that day,
Are fading, fading, memory away.

        "I could easily forget that faint hell,
        In fact I would invite my mind to expel,
        Rumors of fact which lodge in my brain,
        And lie dormant only to return the pain."
Broken bodies populate crusades,
From battlefield to protest, death invades,
All the horrors of war pare down to death,
To screaming people, moaning their last breath.
        "Yet here I stand, no death in sight, but still,
        Alone am I, removed by some will.

"Perhaps I should start searching this space,
	For some clue to my fate in this place."
He looked around once, complete detail,
Like he'd forget something or soon fail,
To remember this spot and where it stood.
He thought of his home in Garadreium Wood,
And other things besides, for with one,
Step came a memory, each detail done,
And presented to his senses complete,
Yet no thought from him did they entreat.

The memories were total and whole,
Each kiss, decoration or scream of a soul.
The moments clear, so clear that new thought,
Was needed not to understand what was brought,
Into his mind, new seemed, yet always there.
Each step signaled a memory flare.
Feeling emotions in sharp detail,
And a battle perceived, every wail.
Like some veil had covered his knowledge,
He now saw clearly with this privilege.

He approached a pool of bluest water,
Where lived a local king's nymph daughter.
Young and rare, naive but learned was she,
Arrol was still in a trance walking free,
When he suddenly lifted his eyes,
To her royal blue orbs, with no surprise.
He knew she was there and waiting for him,
His last memory of a nymph full grim.
"The thoughts of past are complete and done,
	With that time and trouble what have I won?"

"You consider views of your life bothersome?
    Some times in all lives are better from,
    The perspective of distance, yet others,
    Wondrous and joyous lay forgotten,
    Dusty, dry and shriveled mutations,
    Of the mind, that thirsts for the occasion.
    Why is marvel and joy dismissed so?
    Quickly, we can recount collections of woe.
    Think man of this tale of human error,
    'Tis the true grief of man but not his terror.

"The fear of death is terror with mankind,
To rend the heart of anything with mind.
Self preservation was the first command,
Given by God's majesty, glorious grand,
To beasts in proportion to awareness,
Of each life and type with certain fairness.
Sometimes defining the very beast,
And others only a trace like a puzzle piece.
    "Fear you death, Arrol King?" asked the fair Fay,
    "Man am I, and my life my work, each day."

    "But fear you death your own most specific?
    What with your end? Is that not horrific?"
    "Without my life I can no more defend,
    Myself or my life so why fear the end.
    One cannot be, once the spirit flees,
    Yet death may mark my ghost with fearful fees.
    Yet I speak strangely as do you, of time,
    Which shan't catch me just yet in my life prime."
He grinned but caught her countenance,
And serious grew, questions to advance.

"Where is this place? Nothing like it have I,
Ever seen, or somewhere been, in mental fly,
Or in my conquests which carried me,
Far beyond horizons edge by decree."
"This place you've been many moments count,
Both alone and on Garland your bold mount.
Yet this be the first in memory now,
For the others were your dreams or vows.
This place is higher than mind and heart,
Yet more common than any humble start."

"Was I evil, despite my many rights,
Both unsung and in well known fair fights?
From family justice to the public code,
I with myriad virtues closely rode.
Side by each were Garland and Favor,
Virtue's trusty, pure white steed, none braver.
In all my travels I trusted council,
With my right hand support of pure will.
Evil enough from few indiscretions,
For fiery forever with confessions?"

"Merely admitting one's foul evils,
Exorcises them not like red devils,
From the possessed. We must full correct,
Wrongs in every manner, not select,
Our own penance at pleasant moment,
Like lavishing love or much money spent.
You must first right the wrong then pay penance,
Of more than was due, with favor or lance.
Yet no, you are not banished to Dis,
Conscience saved you from the abyss."

"Then blessed bound I your most humble servant,
Unaware was I that grief and torment,
Could grant such a boon unto me unforeseen,
Despite my foul sins and soul true, yet unclean."
"Did you not hear explanations of hell,
And contrition which I was required to tell,
To one with your particular life vow,
For the true test lay ahead, near to now.
Only by a hair have you hell missed,
Yet a lifetime still, and then maybe, bliss.

"For paradise is within your soul grasp,
But race to run with the speed of an asp.
If victory, in whatever form, finds you,
To have true heart and thus grants your full due,
Exalted as a champion on earth,
Your star to grow brighter as well your worth,
And in paradise you shall have content,
In eternity, your life well spent.
For this middle ground is a fighting field,
But here you have not armor, sword or shield."

"What, some war of words, some mental fight,
Before I am released to clear white light?
For dead I am, that is full clear by now,
Never to push the pen or pull the plough,
Again, though I rarely did, 'tis mere pose,
Of one who thought life like a red, red rose.
Of flowers, so perfect in its beauty,
Highly held and defended in duty.
Lovely and most fragrant when considered,
In full aware, yet with mind unlittered."

"Not mental fight must you engage in, but,
    Fight you a physical test and yet what,
    If you refuse such request, then look around,
    This place is unchanging and you are bound,
    Here until the fight is full finished,
    And you have victory or are diminished.
    First you must meet with my father the king,
    He will answer what questions you bring."
She stepped from reeds which surrounded the pool,
And bade him follow rather than be a fool.

The nymph strode with purpose through forgettable,
Land with no feature, not brook to babble,
Nothing to inspire awe or wonder in space,
Or life or time, nothing save the wide waste.
Even near the pool the odd tree did stand,
But as they walked nothing broke the land.
No thing with life could thus be sustained.
By the dead land, death was maintained.
They closed on a steep mound with columns,
Guarding a door, simple pillars, deeply solemn.

    "Enter into the palace," she said slow,
    And swept her hand toward the door, "though,
    Beware of anything you see which moves,
    Save my father the king, who removes,
    The full taint of evil from this place,
    By his actions of justice among the base.
    Leave I must, yet I wish you your desire,
    Now so and do as I bid the time is dire."
She turned and moved away, head down,
    "What is this place," he called, "all around?"

She stopped and lifted her head full prone,
     "This place is the center of the stepping stone."
She then turned and melted out of sight,
Walking into the mindscape and low light.
Arrol faced the door and forced a sigh,
For the threshold of eternity was nigh.
He reached for the door and it swung wide,
At his thought, from which he could no longer hide.
A long hall stretched far, but empty no,
A carnival of characters come and go.

He moved slow through the door as the blind,
Without trust, might attempt feeling to find,
The lost and the new with no help or time.
Each step an adventure a thief and his crime.
A man soon appeared at Arrol's side,
     "What do you seek, my lord? A place to hide?
     I have one to give besides my own,
     Tis very safe setting and strong as stone."
     "I hide not, and I fear not, save the light,
     I advance to the king for talk not flight."

     "Oh brave soul, now talk with king I too,
     Yet still I stayed in limbo, this zoo.
     'Tis better than time without light forever,
     Still the option of fight leaves never.
     Not so good as could be yet better far,
     Than evil and darkness and endless war.
     At peace with myself a rational being,
     Think but a moment before agreeing."
He smiled a wide grin a moment or two,
Ignoring all others in his retinue.

"How might I find the king with whom I deal,
In this matter, before your council congeal?"
"Oh sir, you are held under spell of blue,
The bluest eyes which ever had hue.
The powers will not help, you must fulfill,
Destiny, alone, with only your will.
What interest can she have, a mere spirit?
Love? I think not, like all, they too fear it.
They will test your mind and heart with full fear,
For what? to push you from this peace to tears."

"And yet go on I must, though your words I keep,
To lament your life, but I will not weep.
If all had courage what might courage become,
Certainly no virtue added to one's sum,
Of worth, for if possessed by each and all,
Would be a given, like the round of a ball."
He started away deeper into the mound,
Which inside was like a castle underground.
He wandered past groups which noticed him not,
That he was different from them in thought.

Yet was he so unlike the numerous souls,
Which loitered in limbo without clear goals?
They had faced the throne which he approached,
And spoken with the king, the subject broached.
Many had elected to stay away,
From the field to keep twilight rather than pay,
The price of fear to find a paradise.
Arrol moved through the halls, blood like ice.
Each room he passed fell under his cold stare,
He knew he was looking for destiny's dare.

"Come," said a voice from within the next room,
And he knew it might well spell his very doom.
Yet brave had he been in life not now ended,
For his mind remained, memory mended.
The room was bare except opulent throne,
Which was all the old king had ever known.
To the fields and the fights many came,
But not the king for he wanted no blame,
In arranging battle where the result,
Invariably caused a wide tumult.

All the citizens of this realm lack faith,
In themselves and the king, so become wraiths,
Who fear to fight yet gnash their teeth,
With each victory they might have had, and seethe,
At a loss which sweeps said soul to blackness,
Because the king spelt not the consequence,
To the shadowless soul who fought and fell,
Far, far down into eternity's well.
Thus they stay and populate this empty place,
Fearing to see their folly face to face.

"Come," said the king with a wave, "near to me,
We have some business to discuss free,
And some questions of yours will I field,
Though not ever force you, a sword, to wield."
"First sir, your titles and some guidance,
On which to hail you in circumstance.
For I know not your allegiance, sir,
Though fight, I intend by all that is pure."
"Well said, though I fear you comprehend little,
First, I am KING PELLAS, LORD of the MIDDLE.

"Any title as befits someone of station,
 Is a satisfactory salutation.
 For in this place I am authority, true,
 Yet I simply provide a much larger view,
 Of the universe to all who happen through,
 Of who the latest, last and greatest, is you."
He smiled, inviting Arrol to sit,
They shared a jest and dueled with wits,
 "My liege lord," said Arrol, "why be it so,
 Such a fine man as you is the lord of woe?"

The room hushed and it seemed a shade passed,
And fear settled, yet the effect did not last.
 "Say not that name in these hallowed halls,
 For woe is at the bottom of the river falls.
 Yet that brings more questions, but lay
 Them aside, for my story I will say,
 Once and short but mine, now yours to think,
 On a small northern farm, a boy bought some drink,
 From a peddler which was tainted with death,
 Both the boy's parents drank to no breath.

 "The boy had no thought of poison in the gift,
 But the facts were all given every sift,
 So the boy lived with his mother's mother,
 Until he could work the farm with no other.
 Young and strong he was yet haunted by events,
 Which so affected his life ever since.
 People tried to do things to ease his pain,
 But they were all in error and all in vain.
 He was pleasant to people but in token,
 For he feared having his heart again broken.

"The boy forged an empire from the farm,
And did it without dealing anyone harm,
Yet the tragedy lay heavy on his life,
He protected his heart by not taking a wife.
Though he seemed rich and wise he was not,
For he left love and forgot it's central spot,
In human life for love drives the heart,
Which sharpens the mind causing the limbs to start.
The legs which carry us to the child or lover,
And the hands which caress or tuck in a cover.

"A cycle is love, for that which fuels all,
Is the gratification which prevents stall.
Alas, though now I know, for I was the boy,
Since sent here to preside o'er lack of joy.
Not sin or indiscretion did I commit,
Yet to this post, for folly, do I submit.
Eventually I shall move on ahead,
But not until my former spirit is dead.
Long have I been the king and long shall remain,
A monument to the heart losing to the brain."

"But what the young nymph, your daughter, how so?"
Pellas laughed with mirth, "Another with woe,"
He said between bursts of laughter, "As is mine."
He calmed to the question, "She did incline,
To hide love behind a shield of election,
So fearful was she of personal rejection.
Popularity was her lifelong goal,
Rather than the love of a single soul.
There are many others who reject the notion,
These sons and daughters adopt love's emotion."

"What of this physical test, this field of fight?
Start from the first to explain with insight,
All the polemical possibilities,
Including the qualities and quantities,
Of all involved in typical event."
"You know why it was to here you were sent?"
Arrol nodded, "I can fight for freedom and rest,
If I am victorious in this true test.
But total blackness and fear if I fail,
Yet stay here I can without love or wail."

"If you set the fight, the time is yours to choose,
But I warn you 'tis a fight where one will lose.
Your opponent is set as an equal peer,
Which will require you to harness your fear.
Keep your wits if you are to keep your head,
To the edge of the precipice instead,
Of the land of light and eternal life.
A cataract carries the loser to strife,
With the Lord of Woe who awaits the fallen,
At the canyon's bottom with hatred swollen.

"The battle is found on a small island, Aaon,
Which rises from the river like a crest of dawn,
On water a wake, flat, narrow to the edge,
With stout current sweeping all to the ledge.
So river defines fight and removes the loser,
To the halls of woe and fear's accuser.
The fight is test of strength beyond mere brawn,
Will and true nature of soul show, death be gone.
In this contest there are weapons not, save own
Bodies and minds which learning life has sown.

"Shod and draped simply, yet masked complete,
    For each fighter known by other so compete,
    Because each a representation of all,
    Which is most deadly in the other's fall.
    They met in life, each without satisfaction,
    Though identity could give one thoughtful action,
    And lead to an advantage thus tipping the scale,
    So caution is taken and thus each has a veil.
    This covering totally secured,
    This knowledge is not, by us preferred."

    "Well fight I shall, when all can be prepared?
    Name such time, set the stage, future be dared.
    Though your reception is less than lavish, "
He gestured to the bare room, "I am ravished,
By the attention and honest talk.
Yet I am more anxious to run not walk,
To the battle between souls and true thoughts,
To which my whole life has led and I brought,
By some unseen force, some will, far beyond you,
King Pellas, or anyone here, in vision or view.

"Fight, now, though impossible, must I to hold,
My resolve, my determination bold.
For each moment I wait I grow more pleased,
With simple existence, content, not seized
Allowed to rot within like anything,
Without restraint or compulsion, oh king,
 You have these things which allow you life in hope,
But others, subjects, have found the end of their rope,
And dangle there, held fast, unable to fall,
Or rise and fight for freedom from Middle's pall."

"So fast with the battle dimension, sir,
For it's the only way to effect a cure,
Of the rot which is this place, fear of woe,
Yet any real emotion a telling blow,
Of the space I must flee, for even lament,
To me would be like a light heaven sent."
The king allowed the echoes their due,
Before he spoke, "Arrol, once a king, true,
Your voice and resolve remain unchanged,
Yet your feeling heart is from your soul estranged.

"You cannot trust old passions to react,
The same as they have through your life in fact,
They might rebel against your soul in action.
Your plea revealed new intense emotion,
Which is far from the man of the moment,
You have been when ruled with no repent.
Fight you shall have," he motioned to him,
"Come, we must prepare you," Pellas was grim,
"Caution I beg, or the fight will be short,
Remember, this is a lifetime's effort."

Arrol was arrayed with cloth and shirt,
And shod for good speed and safety from hurt.
White his dress, save a horizontal slash,
Of red o'er the left breast like a gash,
Which merely marked a pocket opening,
With the only display or mark on the clothing.
He was left a short time to find and collect,
His strategy with which he would effect,
His destiny, but of that he thought not,
With the rotting carcass of his life he fought.

"Oh death, thought he, "that void like an open ocean,
Where souls make for some faraway beach or notion.
How can human conscience be held fast?
Docked to the pier of paradise past,
And future in eternal ecstasy lost,
Sundered from that which defines Faust.
Constant bliss would reduce its worth and change,
Heaven to hell and hell to respite full strange.
Life is vibrant and varied thus blessed,
With mutability the engine, best.

"My life has been a chameleon of hues,
Each shade an event too precious to lose,
So memory preserves in the present,
All which has faded both painful and pleasant.
Each minute variation tenacious, clear,
From my moments of triumph to those of fear.
I have tried to extend the grasp of man,
I ordered common affairs into a plan,
Which made life more civilized for all.
When they clamored for a king, I came to the call.

"I dealt fairly with all I saw or judged,
And no reputation did I leave smudged.
Courage I had tempered by compassion,
And true love for all things, after a fashion.
And now death, most despicable to all life,
Which possesses any hope despite strife.
Why a king to this fell place where sport dooms,
One to blackness, where entertainment foul looms,
As the arbiter of eternity whole,
Sport is so fleeting so unlike one's soul.

"Fight? Yes I suppose I must or my years,
In life are but a deathly veil of tears,
And my memory a useless episode,
In the fabric of history left untold.
Some king who ruled between this time and that,
Doing little, really altogether flat.
Well it was legendary for peace, that time,
But little derring-do and no song or rhyme.
That is what they will say if I remain still,
Even defeat to evil will inspire quill.

"Thus fight, in victory or loss guarantee,
Of my immortality in myth to be,
Either great and revered or wicked and fell,
The instrument and incarnation of hell.
Yet lose how? I was honest as any man,
And my deeds beneficial as was my span
Of years which I gave to common peasant,
To improve his lot and make life more pleasant.
Oh, for my life, that precious fragile thing,
Linger yet longer to some slim hope I cling.

"For in my heart full of soul I know of woe,
From petty theft to full pure lies did I sow.
Though never a malicious act did I serve,
The evils of inaction were my reserve.
With Evelyn most dear I called no question,
In fact I dismissed my own suggestion,
That she may have been enchanted by magic,
Not mine but something else much more tragic.
Yet pay I always have in suspicion deep,
Of her devotion within the river sleep.

"Others too, deceptions, but for purpose true,
Directing my actions to the larger view.
Oh try I did but lament still my whole life,
In dealings with each peasant and my wife."
Arrol fell silent, much spoken little said,
No matter for thought because his mind had led,
The discussion through and could not change the sum,
Of each small part taken as true that make numb,
Intricate thoughts of all save the few who see,
Beyond cause and effect, and begin thinking free.

Then a stab of light entered Arrol's space,
A voice rattled his resolve to brace,
"Come now, all is prepared. And you as well?
I pray fair strategy will help you to quell,
What fears still gnaw your sinews of your soul,
For fight will ask every resource in whole."
Arrol was led from the palace to wide pier,
Where a flat boat would spirit him to face fear.
The boat moved calmly through churning cascade,
Of rapids above the falls with no aid.

They moved to the island field from each side,
Arrol saw his opponent's boat glide,
To the isle from the opposite approach,
Similarly clad he was except a broach,
Which held his cloak clasped at the throat.
This rival, Arrol wanted the river to float.
The boats touched ashore and each page said,
"Beware his tricks, or you will be more than dead."
Arrol heard his page but stared full hard,
The voice was pure Pellas, but not the guard.

He took his leave still staring and with a nod,
Slowly turned away feeling full flawed.
Why did a voice strike so suddenly deep,
Into the maw of fear, perpetual sleep?
Still that voice; thought Arrol so he saw not,
The enemy of his good name who he sought.
This man, for man he was, with shoulders broad,
Stood apace with feet apart on the sod,
His eyes cast down and hands clasped behind,
His broad back, yet threat Arrol could not find.

He breathed deep and closed his blue eyes,
The eyes hued as the nymph who never dies.
But Arrol stood oblivious as the boats,
Slipped back into the stream seeming to float,
On air and suggestion, rather than water.
The broach captured Arrol with thoughts of slaughter,
Of armies with weapons he only dreamed,
And every victory, sweeping seemed.
A stone surrounded with wondrous metal,
Intricate, delicate, a flower petal.

The broach an heirloom, the sign of command,
Not of great armies but of a single clan,
Which ruled with fair hand many long lives,
Even with this king whose presence derives,
From a malediction of lament too large,
For he accepted reasons for no tax charge,
From many subjects to the detriment,
Of the kingdom which exists not on sentiment.
Thus this king, Ilore, found himself staring hard,
Wondering which would inspire the historic bard.

Ilore, a gentle man, and peaceful king,
Who never led a charge or had heart to bring,
Violence upon any man who felt that,
There was justice in mercy; because all who sat,
At the table of division and argument,
Are there with a view and reasons to vent.
Ilore had held a sword but bejeweled,
Where rubies red and diamonds brightly dueled.
Yet heavy in his hand it hung, no oneness,
Did man and instrument manage to transgress.

Even the mantle of leadership rested,
Not lightly on Ilore who ever quested,
For the path of least resistance for each
Facet, and issue could present or beseech.
His hands soft yet mind quick, tempered true,
By myriad dealings with subjects who,
Both plebian and patrician did seek,
Matters to be managed around the weak.
So Ilore for his soft heart and honest way,
Found himself in the cascade mist and a fray.

Arrol spied stone of throwing size, two,
So he turned to the slow boat to bid adieu,
And spun to see Ilore engaging the same,
Arrol quickly stooped to a stone to maim.
He released the rock, Ilore unaware,
The missile flew to its destiny there,
And struck with a sickening splash in the river.
Missing Ilore, near, yet making him quiver.
The battle had begun for now each spied,
The other ever and for position vied.

Arrol moved carefully near the second stone,
With a mind to avenge the first weapon thrown.
He moved swiftly but Ilore leapt to fight,
'Fore Arrol could throw, Ilore filled his sight.
They rolled and wrestled till Arrol became bold,
And crushed his opponents jaw and hold,
By directing his forehead to contact bone,
With vicious purpose and answering moan.
As Ilore released his hold, Arrol sprung,
To his feet and kicked, wagging his tongue.

"No fighter are you so foul I must deem,
Attained in life, nothing it would seem.
For fight is but burst of true life force,
Which fuels those on the narrow successful course.
You are soft, so fragile, long a crown prince,
Before king, yet there is little difference,
In your dynasty, for peace reigns ever."
Ilore cowed to the barrage yet never,
Lost his wits so upon Arrol's loss of guard,
Grasped his ankle and pulled full hard.

"Yes unfit and soft I am but clever too,
And like a stone, both in fall and head, are you,"
Laughed Ilore after the heavy thud sounded,
And echoed up the canyon surrounded,
By Arrol's moans and Ilore finding pain,
For each place he touched invoked refrain.
Ilore was more interested in his hurt,
Than following his gain with a fighting spurt.
Arrol crawled to his feet with glaring eyes,
And realized that the gentle needs be wise.

Arrol spent some time circling, gaining strength,
Ilore remained motionless at length,
His back to the river within one stride,
The isle of Aaon now host to the pride,
Of two general ways of conducting life,
Embodied in their handling of strife.
Then Arrol struck with a lunge at Ilore's chest,
But the defender was ready, so equal to test.
He moved away, first back, drawing Arrol,
On to the brink where he hit like a barrel.

Ilore leapt upon the floundering fool,
Holding him under to protect his jewel,
Of achievement, the peaceful reign of a king,
Where violent death is never caught loitering.
Still a sickly feeling ran up his arm,
Like a deep chill that can never be warm,
But hold on he did till the body fought not,
Then feeling the victor he rose on the spot.
Arms in the air, wondering why only silence,
Greeted champions? Was it his use of violence?

The onlookers saw the body rise but Ilore,
With back turned was unaware Arrol bore,
Him hostile intent, but the possum rose,
From his near doom and fear of all his woes.
Ilore heard the water move and was shocked,
How had he failed? He felt that destiny mocked,
His hopes to come clean in this event.
As Arrol came toward him his full will went,
He wondered if he could try to kill again,
And his memory caused a shuddering strain.

Ilore backed away from Arrol's advance,
Too shocked and confused for fighting stance.
Back, back he moved with eyes fixed straight,
The precipice loomed. Ilore tempted fate.
Still steadily back no notice of doom,
Ilore was swiftly running short of room.
Arrol wrestled with the thought of stopping,
To prevent Ilore from retreating and dropping,
From Aaon and honorable victory,
For victory Arrol felt a near tick to be.

He stopped for true honor but Ilore not,
For fear flared eyes by the broach were caught.
As he approached the very brink Arrol leapt,
One foot felt empty space but Arrol kept,
Ilore from falling, "Hold me and help your cause."
But Ilore felt fight was hopelessly flawed,
In no physical contest could he excel,
Almost resigned to an eternal hell,
Ready to cast himself into the chasm deep,
But Arrol refused such victory cheap.

With a mighty heave he bore Ilore clear,
Of the edge and walked away from his peer.
He turned, "For honorable resolution,
Of this single affair, not an evolution,
Of my character but desire to defeat,
You within the bounds of honor I entreat,
You to heed my words and prepare your defense."
    "It would seem defeat is my only recompense,
    For an act, such as I have just witnessed.
    I wonder if I would have passed the same test?"

The words weighed heavily on Ilore true,
He silently vowed reciprocal view,
Yet Arrol set to fight till one only,
Remained on the grassy plain lonely,
Yet victorious and exalted by all,
With the fruit of a life no longer small.
Though both battered, the battle just begun,
And much lay ahead to be all lost or won.
Ilore shook his apprehension far away,
And Arrol faced him tired of delay.

A rivulet of blood ran down Arrol's arm,
And his legs showed many red spots of harm,
His cloak torn partly away by his prey,
But still shod with mind sharp he held sway,
Over Ilore, the wretch whose tattered cloak,
No more a mantle fair than 'twas a joke.
The broach still held only collar and pocket,
Yet Arrol stared at the detailed locket,
For now he saw in the ornate gold clasp,
A figure which made him, a warrior, gasp!

For a horse, a mare, stood still upon a plain,
But no simple prairie stand, this horse without reins,
Proud, bold this horse, this great Garland young, yet old.
For Garland it was, his likeness not grey but gold,
And near a notched spear with stylized light,
Radiating golden power in peace or fight.
Endurendil the scepter of Arrol King,
With the scar of his misuse of the thing.
Arrol aghast of these symbols his house had,
Such effrontery served to drive him mad.

Arrol ignored his own blood and Ilore's too,
Even though one was red and the other blue.
Ilore's wounds confined to torso alone,
Like the deep cut which displayed a hip bone.
Blood had drained from his face and gathered,
In a small pool or two where they were fathered.
Arrol straightened and relaxed his guard,
But only an instant then soon he hit hard,
Again Ilore was taken in by the ploy,
But in this honorable fight Arrol found joy.

Like an animal without conscience, savage,
He fought, tearing with nails in violent ravage,
Of everything around Ilore, green grass and stone,
Paid for harboring him and were rent to atone.
Arrol's wrath knew only the bounds a man
Had in weaponless state where rage will and can.
And more blood came from wet wounds further torn,
Soon a blood red blanket did the ground adorn,
Ilore fought to defend and remove the fiend,
And wondered whose hands would have to be cleaned.

He tried to rise as Arrol came spent,
But he fell back, body full of deep rents.
Ilore felt his open hand close round a rock,
As he tried to rise again between knocks,
He brought the mass into contact with aggression,
Determined to make a long lasting impression.
The force of the blow caused strange sensation,
To run through Ilore's arm post demonstration.
Arrol staggered straight and life force ran red,
Down his face like a delta -- direction dead.

The blow like a balm to Ilore's wounds,
For he no longer was faint enough to swoon.

    "Fool, thou art, loathsome creature of despite,"
Spake Ilore, "Deal with animals for they fight,
As you, contrary to a gentleman's code,
But with a necessary passion and mode.
Every advantage you crave and employ all,
Yet when handed victory you balk, because my fall,
Accords you too little honor in history.
You are a massive inconsistent mystery."

Spake Arrol, "And thou, who now condemns, should be,
For who would fight an immortal soul to free,
Yet never lift an angry hand save to save,
Immediate pain or your heirloom from grave?
And what of said broach? Some strength you seem to gain,
With it, I leap where the powerful refrain,
And the powerless find fear and cannot think,
Of deliverance so they find solace with drink.
You who strike only in simple self defense,
Has left me gravely hurt but with much expense."

    "Yes, I lay in this pool of mine own fair force,
    Which drains away providing the pall a source.
    But as I speak your color changes and orbs fix,
    And I deem this is not another of your tricks."
With that Arrol began to stagger with weight,
From some source not seen, for his blood loss great.
Like a man with much grape and all reason spent,
To and fro wavered red trail where he went.
Toward the water he made for he resigned,
To noble loss with which honor does incline.

Ilore sat up at the sight, "No!" he cried,
"I am beaten, unable to defend or hide."
The body floated slowly by, face to the sky,
With bloodied water following the lie.
The waterfall roared louder now as Arrol,
Lifted one hand to the vaulted sky in farewell,
To all his hopes and schemes in wonder,
For failure would exact the cost and sunder,
Him from his dreamed of fate, eternal glory.
Still Arrol thought of his life and wasn't sorry.

He would be yet known as a companion to woe,
So he thought of others known as joy's foe,
And realized those people like him, complete,
Not purely moral nor fully unjust, but discreet.
With words and favors they seek to wander,
Through life with a dream to be history's ponder.
The roaring broke into his thought, it was near,
But now he felt there was little to fear.
Ilore dragged his broken body not far,
He knew that he could not reciprocate the honor.

Victory! thought Ilore yet the word near dead,
For he poured his hope on the ground as he bled,
Would he be delivered when the cataract claimed,
The victim and might he then be named?
Ilore wondered most if he would survive,
Until the river launched its flotsam to dive,
Into the vast gorge of woe far, far below.
Closer, closer to the very edge his foe,
Found solace with death in life for the first time,
While he was content he now knew his true crime.

Why did he forever rationalize action,
Knowing he wasn't joining his heart's faction?
Pure virtue became blind to immediate gain,
While flesh never hurt his conscience felt the pain.
Had his heart not held such division he felt sure,
He would have labored less in life to cure,
The ills of morality, the curse of some,
And salvation, for others a plumb.
But for this deep defect different would be days,
Of both life and death in a myriad of ways.

A fair swallow in flight swooped through Arrol's sight,
But growing gloom obscured the full view in spite.
The river quickened as it spilled down,
The last steps to doom and ambition's crown.
When Arrol felt this speed he cast his eyes,
Back to the isle, back to Ilore to surmise,
Why were they two tied together by the wise,
Or powers, or providence, and why disguise?
The fowl found its way to the Aaon shore,
Where Ilore thought it an omen to implore.

    "Come now fair fowl the dire deed has been done,
    And I somehow have weathered all and won.
    Reveal yourself and heal my horrible wounds,
    For in accordance with the test, I await boons,
    Promised me by Pellas king, with survival,
    Which is moments away barring revival,
    Of my opponent and better at battle,
    Though distant cousin, in speech, witness my prattle."
With that the swallow lunged at Ilore's head,
Removed his mask and without a word, fled.

Arrol watched the bird all along its flight,
It robbed Ilore and Arrol kept it in sight.
Ilore saw Arrol follow the swallow's path,
But Arrol swung his gaze as he fell to wrath.
For one terrible second when momentum held,
Arrol above the chasm their stares did meld,
And down he fell for seven nights and mornings,
Past many multitudes of evil warnings.
Yet his last vision fixed forever unchanged,
'Twas a mirror image though deeply estranged.

Ilore knew not the brave turn of perspective,
Awarded the fallen though not defective,
For the face left unprotected and fame free,
Now found solace with one hand to infamy.
Ilore saw the last wide eyed shock which lent,
Itself to pain as much as surprise spent,
He saw the vault of sky slide to reveal stars,
Together morning and evening, Venus and Mars.
The swallow shed the mask in the fast river,
And alighted on Aaon as life giver.

With wounds staunched and strength revived,
Ilore rose to greet fair swallow who arrived,
With the wind beat of wings but approached slowly
As a man, "I have been engendered wholly,
To perform and speak at this test which brought,
You to this special place where souls pure are sought.
But the departing souls must work to maintain,
The true nature this test allows them to attain."
He spoke to Ilore direct and others around,
On both sides of the canyon did souls abound.

"Tis said a man enters and leaves this life,
With nothing, every man with or without a wife,
Leaves a legacy of life always large,
No matter which station the future his charge.
If common folk he bridges a generation,
With knowledge of years he finds veneration.
His contribution more collective as years,
Pass to generate a history of tears.
For few societies feel contemporary
Time is a golden age, rather they are wary.

"The noble bear a burden of similar size,
But they are fewer who implement and advise.
Thus legacy singular each man renown,
For deeds in virtue or despite alone,
This plight of kings and curse which haunts them.
How to balance death with life from which it stems?
T   hose of deeds cannot hide within the mass of men,
Because they lead, because they are never told when,
Or how to handle the issues large or small,
They stand each, individual, or they fall.

"Would that man could relieve his soul of all,
He was and stood for with a stroke as small,
As his own death, where would pure purpose be,
In that race to live and find true destiny?
But what of the crown of love, a baby's birth,
Where two can share with their creation in true mirth?
A child from its first moment on this Earth,
Has the gift of humanity and instant worth,
He also has a whole heritage direct,
From his fore bearers which no one can select.

"All enter this life with much to their good,
But most know not their goals yet they should.
They focus their lives to security,
And ignore the wild call of heart's purity.
They wander and wonder in futility,
Never scratching the surface of their ability.
We can, only with death, lament this horror,
For horror it becomes, a life spent in error.
With this victory you can help to save,
Others from this fate with the pure virtue they crave.

"Only few can you help, so choose those close,
To mistake who are like to benefit, with dose,
Of reality seen uncensored in youth,
As you have just witnessed in virtuous truth.
Greed nor gain for said sake will advance your life,
Cause you wear away your shoulder with fears rife.
Come now son, you can pursue which ever dreams,
Your heart fancies though your imagination teems,
With thoughts and projects you cannot number,
Not one of them will another encumber."

His voice hung in the quickly clearing air,
As he came to flight no longer a man there,
Just the tattered shoulder and pocket section,
Of a simple bloody cloak caught in reflection.
The illuminated breast with a bloody swath,
Of violence cut vertically through the cloth,
Lay forlorn and forgotten but a symbol still,
Of hope and human spirit with unwavering will.
Now Aaon waited for wanderers in wonder,
To come together 'fore they are cast asunder.

As he fell Arrol chanced upon a thought,
"Finally I will find what I have always sought,
I arrive conquered by my own pretense.
Yet among such souls my joy of space is immense.
Each of us full resigned to fatal flaw,
So our minds clear and senses no longer raw.
Woeful only in lack of direction true,
Yet pleased to be party to a larger view.
But not changed or reformed these souls stay,
In constant exercise of their chosen way."

Arrol flared across the heavens out of sight,
Yet his passing again left the sky dark at night,
The final flash of reality provided,
Proof that the combatants could not be divided.
Arrol worked for full immediate gain,
With no thought to the future's bold refrain.
"Prepare for history to rot effort away,
If tomorrow is to be ruled by today,
Then yesterday must consider the now and then,
And all must draw strength from the eventual when."

These characters which move confusedly through,
All of life's wild wonderment wishing they knew,
Of reason, of hope and of dreams not a few,
Stand open mouthed at times' changing hue.
They blunder along reaching for high blue sky,
Thinking progress better than simply standing by.
But people will not see they occupy a place,
Usually because they love the very space.
Dreaming of this and that, mere material passion,
But contentment of the mind is not in fashion.

At what type of price do we each lesson learn,
A cost constant or variable, can we discern?
Are such things tied to a true value instead?
So dearly paid lessons should cause no dire dread.
One experience can have effects profound,
In many ways to many people all around,
Minute matters, in retrospect, can be,
Turning points, which nobody ever really sees.
Some men make a thought their abiding principle,
And think that thought makes them invincible.

The tale of one true man comes to an end,
Yet those connected to him will ever contend,
That the tale never ends it simply becomes,
More complex, adding to it the multiple sums,
Of every life which touched or turned it,
From Evelyn and Kevin to a humble poet.
Everyone wants a piece of immortality,
Though it be not there, but under some tree.
For 'tis true immortality is wasted,
On some dead who have it, but never taste it.

With nothing save his ambition Arrol gained,
Wealth, power and for his courage was famed.
Letting nothing deviate his rise to success,
He gained the world and yet still regressed.
His quest for fame consumed the truth and him,
At first his flame burned brilliant but now dim.
All battles are laced with legendary tales,
Of courage, selfless bravery and heroes,
Who have gone with the dead to the vast halls of Dis,
For memory of violence cannot be bliss.

My toil now transhifted, the tale told complete,
I reserve only time to make good my retreat.
This story of length should allow an escape,
To all problems and woes such as the grape.
Though I know not if it is as a pleasant sip,
Or like the horror of the new sun's mental grip.
Still, some will find a moment or two might move,
While others will never find reason to approve.
For they would obliterate the rhythm and rhyme,
Defining as ridiculous the sublime.

All men have been touched by temptation some time,
To commit a temporal or spiritual crime.
And though some claim to hold no god supreme,
They still pray for luck when they plan to scheme.
Clean conscience on all matters in a life,
Is as pleasant as difficult, so thus to strife.
Each soul has a portion which to reconcile,
For mankind cannot his own soul defile.
So each soul must define what is just,
Without which we are but a handful of dust.

END

Prose version - A Wander Within Wonder

Part One - Endell's Song

Welcome my friends to this telling of an ancient story.

It is a fable with a multitude of characters. Most of these people are simply living their lives, content to keep the darkness at bay, rejoice in their small successes and work to master their talents, improve their skills and find what victories in life that they can.

But one among them defies this approach to life.

He is a man who finds himself a blank slate, thrust into life, who faces the demands of his story, and who is fully formed at the start of our tale because it is only then that it truly begins.

This ancient story is fashioned by the mind and mouth of he who knows the tale, and whose perspective on the events shapes the way they are told. You the reader may see other things in the tale.

The tale is told by one who has told stories before and will tell more in the future. Some of these stories are well conceived, deftly told and satisfying to the listener. Others are less successful, obtuse to the listener and find the audience unable to absorb them, or, are so fractured by abstraction that they are difficult to understand.

Tales and telling are difficult things to master, audiences are fickle and the same tale can be a pleasure for some to hear and a misery for others.

Tales are often about simple things like day and night, or like the passage of time. Other stories take on larger canvases and are laid across the vastness of space, or deal with the wonder of the four seasons, or the personality and legitimacy of kings. They might speak of the nature of flora and fauna, and touch upon the creation of the world, its wonders and even detail how the world and all upon it became the way it is today.

As this tale is told, the teller is thinking about the future, the legacy of his own life, and what happens at death and what might be faced in an afterlife, if such a thing exists. The teller and the reader should consider if religion spares us our fears? We all wonder if human reason can quell these fears?

And before we delve into this tale we must acknowledge that while life is lived in each moment, it is also lived with a knowledge of the past and an expectation of a future. That is the baggage of the here and now that everyone carries with them. It is what makes tales live in the universal experience or die among the road not followed by history.

People only have a finite amount of time to sort out their lives. With enough time a person could know almost every-thing he has access to. And with that knowledge he could understand evil and perhaps triumph over it. But people do not have unlimited time.

****

So help me to remember my tale. And if I be so lucky as to complete it, perhaps it will lend me some credence in your eyes or value in my life and beyond it.

I have already written about growth, love, fear, pain and the scary path one must take to success and pleasure.

Until now most of my concerns have been specific and considerations short in duration, points to be made rather than anything deeper. I have put in my practice at telling tales. While I am not always completely successful, but I am ready for a larger canvas and broader themes, even if my skill might require stretching in order to become as advanced as other tellers of tales.

This story concerns our world of men and the connection of our lives to something more, the divine world that we often speculate upon. It concerns man's desire for power and material wealth, and the often ignored desire for spiritual riches.

Everyone on Earth has these desires, to gain comfort and safety, as we start our lives with nothing and work towards having all our desires on Earth. We too often forget that this life is short, and in many ways, it is a lead up to eternal life, so our temporal world is not the only thing we concern ourselves with.

We battle our way seeking truth and beauty as part of our search for what is required of us. Everyone everywhere has these concerns, but they are not important once we pass to the next world, we need to learn the truth of that, so we can be free of the need for material possessions and that measurement of our temporal   success.

And now my tale.

****

He lay silently on the grass, apparently asleep.

The green lawn was perfectly clipped, manicured, and it sloped down to a stream. Dawn was near, the sky alight and a thick mist rose all around, obscuring the distance.

He was tall and strong, noble in bearing but he lay quiet with the stream passing by silently, without ripple or splash. Trees, fed by the watercourse, shaded him as the sun rose. As it did, he too awoke and became aware.

He was new, unblemished, fully green in his maturity, and knew not this place where he was. It was a place of wonder, bathed with magic but full of expectation and beauty to mask its unsettled nature. What might come next, none could tell, it would come from the heart of his lost soul.

This mighty man lay still until the sun worked its way up in the sky and shone on him, casting its light past the shade trees. At the gathering warmth he awoke his limbs. And naked, and he blinked and stretched to feel his own power, the sinew of his muscles, the bending of his joints and that which his own being controlled.

He sat up and saw only a bit of mist still above the stream. His blank mind formed a single thought.

"I am Endell. I've been lost but now I am found."

He rose to his feet and felt the power of his body, the strength of his legs and arms, the suppleness of his movements. Given the damage he could inflict upon the grass and trees he knew he was a master, a strong, agile warrior, not intended to allow things to happen to him, but instead someone whose initiative made things happen to his advantage.

He ran about, taking pride in his power and abilities. He could distantly remember himself, the feelings of his body and a singular consciousness. What was he? He knew he was intended for renown, to have his name and his visage inspire anyone who came upon him.

But what should he do, alone and loitering in mist. He ran down to the stream and understood its flow. That water must be coming from somewhere and going somewhere, he thought.

"The water is running away from something, something bad and frightening. I want to test myself," he thought, and started upstream.

Following the stream Endell wandered along for a time, noting the trees, the brush, the grass and the running water. When his way was barred he would take to the stream bed, walking or wading against the current until he could find a path.

Soon Endell chanced upon a man dressed in gray. Hidden in the trees, Endell watched him silently. The grey clad man took off his clothing to bathe in the stream. It was then that

Endell realized he was naked. He understood that clothes were necessary and he moved quietly to where the clothing lay. Endell silently moved to the man's cart, grabbed the clothing, unhitched his horse from the cart and moved off slowly at first to cover his deed.

He never heard a sound or word of complaint and soon forgot about the man in the stream and the nasty surprise that awaited him.

Endell left the cart so the man had most of his possessions. He thought himself clever and noble to only take what he needed.

Once they had put some distance away from the stream, Endell encouraged the horse to gallop and it did, immediately, with a joy at having abandoned the cart, and testing its full speed.

"Garland, I shall call you," said Endell aloud as he stroked the horse's mane. "Do my bidding and you shall have your measure of freedom."

Garland whinnied loudly, and though it scarce seemed possible, picked up his pace, giving Endell a peace as he had released this horse from the torment of the cart. He thought it was obvious that this horse was never meant for a plodding farmer's pace, it had the heart of a warrior.

The gray steed, matched its new master in look and outlook. As a visual they were unchanged, two plodding agricultural workers, but in motion they showed an aggressive powerful visage.

Endell let Garland choose the pace. They rode hard as the sun burned off the fog and morning dew. They kept riding hard until the sun dappled the treetops with fading light. Garland was free and had reserves of energy needing to be released after years of being tied to a cart.

They kept moving until there was no light left before turning off the path and finding a small dell with a few sheltering trees. There they sheltered.

In the morning they woke to face a large forest spread out before them unseen in the darkness of their approach. Turning to look, Endell saw they had crossed a wide grassland. He faced the forest, his arms wide to embrace it, the possibilities it contained, the unknowns, the fair and the foul, all called to him. The ancient beauty of the woodland filled his vision and his future.

Endell encouraged Garland to move into the wood, and as they moved he gazed about him in wonder. Only streaming, stark shafts of light penetrated the canopy. The leaves and branches kept out the general daylight, rendering the wood magical with columns and beams of light here and there providing enough definition between the shadows and the light that Endell and Garland could find their way.

The trees appeared to glow according to their age. Young saplings beamed with light while hoary old trees with cracked bark gave off a barely perceptible light, like a day-light moon. As they got deeper in the forest, the canopy closed off the sunlight leaving the light of the trees as the only viable way to navigate. Soon it became apparent that while young trees glowed strongly, youthful trees were the brightest and at some point older trees began to shed less light.

They crossed many a stream, and moving up and down ravines and soft valleys and dales, which had the affect of confusing their direction as there was no path to follow or sunlight by which to navigate.

Endell knew this wood somehow. It vaguely lived in his deepest knowledge, not as a memory but more as a general understanding, like his ability to breathe and see and walk.

It was Garadreium Wood, its name from before memory, allowed people to wander, but only as visitors. The forest was supreme. Those who could co-exist with the wood, giving its ways a pass and living in peace with it, wandered about for years in happiness. Others might find themselves lost, bat-tling the wood, constantly wary of its traps, fearful of their lives for just as long. The forest's malevolence was not displayed as violence but rather control of the future and as a fuel to the despair of those who could not escape.

Those who lived in the wood or near it, knew of tales that told that its center contained a mythical pool, the Mithomere. This pool was an oracle for those who gazed upon it, telling of future events, reading the dreams and hopes of those who looked into its depths, and reflecting their evil or fair countenance and thoughts. It was said that a ripple across the pool during your vision was especially portentous as the pool understood mixed hopes and torn dreams, and its illusions could be affected by the ripple in thought.

The forest itself was impossible to understand as pathways forked and bent away from what appeared as a straight and true path. In some cases expected destinations were empty, hollow places. And through the wood there were various creatures, wild and tame, fair and foul. A witch here, a troll there. Travelers might find a confidence man one day and a devil the next or be welcomed into a fair town or village. The entire forest was alive, awake and striving for its desires of the moment. It waited and watched looking for a chance to take advantage of a fool, of a guard let down, of an error.

But there were precious wonders in Garadreium Wood too. Despite that, wariness was rewarded and wonders rare by comparison.

Garland and Endell entered the wood with care, vigilant, following a streambed they had chanced upon. There was a path near the water and they used it, always aware of keeping the water close to their right. Without knowing why, Endell expected to be challenged, expected anger and opposition to their travel.

They picked their own path, staying so close to the water that the trees began to close them in, and the brambles became so thick that they decided to take a different approach. Endell dismounted and took up a large stick and began hacking away at the undergrowth, beating a path for them while remaining within sight of the river.

He quickly noticed that the brambles were tough as they tried to move toward the river. But if he tried to move away from the river, he was able to brush them aside more easily. Soon, he had lost sight of the river, and then he could no longer hear its flow. He considered trying to move back towards it. As he considered his effort he blundered out onto a worn pathway, narrow but distinct. He decided to follow it, hoping to find a formal road.

"Why are we being pulled this way?" he said aloud. Garland merely looked at him, willing to be led.

In his mind Endell turned over the reasons. Paths can direct fools to follow where they do not want to go, as the way is easier, but not true to a chosen destination. He decided that this minor path should lead to a more formal roadway, one carved through the forest. He did mull over the idea that the road he was looking for might not provide the destination he wanted. But to know that would require him to take the road and find out. Going back through the pathway he had beaten through the undergrowth back to the start of his adventure, was not an option as it led to nowhere and nothing, failing to advance his story.

Endell decided the road was preferable as he had no fixed destination and he would take his chances on the destination the road provided. He knew that his future could be glorious or horrible no matter what path he chose. But it gnawed at him that the direction of the road represented a destiny that appeared to be chosen for him. He could not stop wondering why he was being pulled along to some fate, pulled away from the path he himself had chosen. And pulled away due to his unwillingness to battle the difficult elements that stood in his way.

Garland whinnied, sensing his master's uncertainty, which had come upon him suddenly after hours of determined travel though difficult ways. The gentler path did not seem like a good choice but rather a weakness, a failure of direction.

And still the great horse, cantered forward, confident in each step, that any danger would be seen and met as necessary. Once past this crisis of choice, Endell took on his steed's approach, wary of eye, but confidently marched on with a purpose to his step, even if that purpose was simply to take the next step, and the next, and the next.

It was the only way he could move ahead. The only way to get ahead.

To continue Endell realized he must remain strong. The forest was manipulating his efforts. He wanted desperately to get away from this place, even if it was to another, similar place, he just wanted to believe the choices were his own.

The path they were on was narrow, not much more than a track, in many places seeming to disappear only to reappear when the ground forced only one line of travel. Rocks, slopes and large trees and their roots gave direction of the path, straight there, winding here.

In the straight sections Garland picked up speed, as if there was a visible foe to meet and Endell was unburdened by fear or confusion. He knew his destiny was to fight, to strive. They moved more and more rapidly along the narrow path, through branches and leaves that overhung it, breaking some of the smaller ones with a snap.

Sleep did not appear to be required within the confines of the forest, so strange its state. Travelers were able to continue on or rest as they saw fit. The strangeness of the wood was held in disguise by a sprinkling of random roses in various shades, daisies and other flowers, creeping vines and majestic trees.

The woodland built these scenes to disguise the truth of its potentially fatal nature. Some people would die within its borders.

There were eyes looking at all that passed, creatures in thrall to the forest and other nameless things which collectively were more than a match for Endell to take on. Individually these things were barely even noticed by him.

And then his narrow path opened on a wider way, one he had expected through the wood. At the junction was a pavilion and within was a maiden who was not startled by his explosion through the branches.

"Glory and gold or giants greed to see, which way wouldst though go gladly, brave sir? You can ask me three questions to gain your clues but only one will I answer true."

The maid fell silent as a stone, and as hard. She had faltered on this road and had found herself fated to guard it. Meeting this maid, Endell realized that he and his steed were drawing closer to danger.

The silence grew as Endell contemplated his situation and options. The maiden appeared to have turned to stone, awaiting his queries. Only the soft thrush of the high leaves in the trees could be heard to mark the time. There was no breeze upon the forest floor.

"I do not want safety if it means my liberty is restricted. I will not require your help if two-thirds of it is more than useless. I shall continue east in the direction of this road pursuing the rising sun as my guide as the canopy allows. And as the sun rises I shall also rise to greet any honorable men I meet," he said.

Endell reigned Garland to leave, moving east, unsure of what he might find, a monster or other danger or some true help along the way.

The damsel tried to scream, but she was barely able to creak out a call for help, bound by her fate.

"Now that you have defied my purpose, the spell of my slavery is partly broken and I can flee this fate. But I will be pursued, and I know not the shortest way. Please escort me from this place and lead me to my fate."

"No lady," said a grim Endell, "I seek evil and want to test myself by facing it down. So we can leave, but we will not run. If taking you will find me a fight against evil, then come, we will go together."

She took a place upon Garland at Endell's invitation, but warned him to heed her tale and find a good defense to employ.

Endell laughed quite merrily, " Lady your fate is my first trial. And while I am not sure what my ultimate quest will be, I am confident my story will not end here with you."

Having no choice at who would champion her cause she tried to hold back her surprise at his confidence.

"How will you win over evil when you are weaponless, have no defensive armor and appear by your clothes to be a simple farmer? Perhaps you are a very simple farmer."

"We will cross that span when necessary, when I see what stands in our way and we are both convinced it will not yield."

Endell explained that he was ready for anything, a giant slavering monster, or a menacing tall giant, or a black rider moving deliberately against them. Even the malevolence of the forest itself would be opposed.

They cantered all day, eventually settling down for a rest, the maiden using a leaf covered willow root on which to rest her head while Endell kept watch. He dosed and as dawn flecked the forest growth the maiden awoke and screamed as the root had seized her.

"The evil has found us," she choked out the words.

Endell leapt to the ready, grasping a dead branch and wedging it up under the root using the ground to gain leverage to free the maid. As it moved only a touch, he forced a flat rock into the space and then reinserted the branch lever over the rock and applied more force. He could feel the root give, and then it split, freeing the maid and leaving Endell to wonder at the nature of the evil he faced.

"Brave you might be, but do not be a fool. The evil grows and it follows us closely."

"If that's the worst your curse can produce I feel very safe and so should you," Endell said.

"Take it not lightly sir. We are marked. The evil will grow. Who knows how far we must travel to escape it."

Endell threw back his head and laughed unworried by her screed.

"I fear men who are that proud," she said unnerved by his derision as he continued to look merrily upon her. "I appreciate your confidence but you still look more like a farmer than not."

Garland finished grazing and nosed up to Endell in the middle of this discussion. Upon the maid's words Garland snorted his own derision. They might look like rural folk but he knew the road and knew that their way was hard and heavy. And he too, knew that they would win renown from city folk, townspeople and farmers too.

No farmer's nag was he, this horse was to be a great steed, together with Endell a force of renown, with great tales following their deeds.

The maid turned to Garland and smiled as she could read his mind. She reached out and stroked his neck. She was taken by the horse and its attitude and felt lighter of heart and foot once she climbed him to ride.

They left the willow without further issue but it soon found their concerns doubled. Two heavily hided beasts, huge with long snouts of teeth, ran at them on four legs, rising up on their hind legs as they approached.

The beasts confronted the mounted horse, staying low to disguise their size. Their long narrow heads had eyes on each side, allowing them sightlines of almost a complete circle about them,. However these widely spaced eyes produced poor depth perception all around and directly forward and behind them it was best, but it forced them to roll and loll their heads around to gain a better view. It was a menacing effect, but somehow Endell knew this was their weakness.

Endell thought, if he was a knight, and blessed with a knights garb and weapons, he would rush the beasts with his sword. Despite their thick hides they were soft underneath and had trouble fixing sight on him if he moved quickly.

But he was weaponless. So he got off Garland at a distance, found some stones and threw them hard, finding eyes or near enough, with his first two throws. Now one-eyed, each beast could barely perceive him and they backed away to preserve only a defeat rather than their deaths. Complete blindness would have accomplished the same thing a sharp sword or lance might.

While Endell gathered and threw, the maid had found a stout, straight stick which she sharpened on a large rock to a ready point.

Endell knew he would continue to fight in any course but when she presented him with the rough lance he knew with certainty that fate was on his side. He chased at the beasts, inflicting painful stabs, but left them as they trundled away, trailing blood in their path.

Now with a weapon, Endell took to Garland, pleased that he could defend them. Yet the maid felt cornered by evil intentions closing in on them and did not share Endell's confidence. But with no other means to flee she believed she was tied to this farmer and his grey horse.

They moved deeper into the wood at a good pace and faced nothing more dangerous than the morning dew.

The world they inhabited and travelled through seemed simple enough, with trees and their path and an occasional garden of flowers and vines, apparently planted and tended by some unseen denizen of the wood. From the single tree they had encountered with an evil root the forest had presented itself as unpredictable and a reservoir of malevolence and bubbling violence. Round every bend they looked keenly for something to confront, something that might challenge them, or vengeful sprites that would bar their way. However with each step Endell became bolder. And all the while the maiden worried more deeply, knowing their next challenge was creeping up on them.

"My fair lady, I am without my manners. Please speak with soft speed your name, before I am forced to guess at it."

She lifted her gaze and wistfully gained mastery over her fear, "Evelyn. My name is Evelyn."

He laughed, and again when she appeared shocked, "I should have guessed that," he mocked, "and maybe I would have too, if you had forced me to guess."

She knew he thought himself clever seeing the pun in her name, but knew that she had no evil in her, so she decided to turn the tide of his mirth.

"And of names, dear sir, do you have one?"

"Aye, 'tis Endell, and not a pun."

"Mine is the name I gained at birth," Evelyn said, "Though your joking makes it seem given in mirth. Not so rarefied your wit but if you wear it, it should fit. And Endell, your name, is majestic beyond you, with your farmer's bearing and homespun things."

She said that if Endell was his name she would honor it and address him as was his wish, but she prophesied that one day in the future he would answer to Arrol. She decided that was a more fitting name for him but would not say why.

They plodded along during this conversation, seeking neither speed nor stealth. Soon they came up to a turn in the broad path, forgetting their vigilance at things unseen while in conversation. The turn would soon dispel them of that mistake.

Swinging around the curve, a wide river came into view crossing the road. Garland halted at the sight of it, still some distance away. It was too wide and appeared too fast running for him to safely cross. They warily approached this obstacle.

Endell spied a ferryman. As they approached him he stood beside his flat bottomed boat, with its name 'Lady Anne' on the bow. That he was old was evident, but he not wrinkled, and his skin fair. It was his eyes that belied his age. They were moving, moving like the river, darting from horse to man, from man to woman, from woman to lance. This was no ordinary group of travelers, he thought.

"Say you, Ferryman, can we cross this torrent?"

An unusual question as that was obviously his purpose, so the Ferryman declined to answer and sought details of the travelers instead.

"By whose will and for what purpose are you sent?"

"I and my steed to find our destiny. And young Evelyn, whom I protect, safety of a kind."

"That is strange speech from a farmer," said the Ferryman though he knew the wood to be haunted and the people in it, odd.

The Ferryman said he would take them across but warned them not to touch the red water as it was enchanted and could cause any manner of reaction and delay.

"A single drop in the right place can overwhelm you. Be careful until we reach the other side, when you will set foot upon my employer's land and realm.

They boarded the boat and the ferryman pushed off. As he did the current broke. The stream turned to glass, calm, smooth and easily navigated.

Endell and his party did not flinch at the change, but took note as it was dramatic and unexpected. They said nothing to each other or the Ferryman.

A green fish broke the surface some distance from the boat, but the splash was well away from them. The maiden moved to the far side of the boat for safety from the water, but a second fish crested the surface, this time quite near the boat, and caused a drop of water to fall on Evelyn's lips.

Her eyes grew wide with the shock and the fear and then the magic of the water took hold and she slowly fell backwards.

She fought hard against the motion but she could not stop it nor cry out at her danger. All her effort to warn Endell of her situation produced only a sigh and she tumbled off the boat and into the red river water.

Endell immediately made to dive in, but she surfaced with a smile, flat on her back, eyes wide open, seemingly buoyed up high in the water. Taking care not to touch the water, Endell grabbed her clothing. It was dry. He braced against the gunwale and with great strength lifted her out of the river and back into the boat.

She seemed to find her own consciousness and clung to him, giving him a kiss as he held her, while he was trying to find a safe place to put her down.

The river swelled up at the theft of its victim, swirling and speeding, the current throwing them left and right. The ferryman was powerless to stop the current as it over-whelmed his ability to pole the boat through the stream. They were carried far down the river away from their landing and deep into the Garadreium Wood.

After a time the river slowed but they were miles from the crossing and had no chance to move back to find the road on the opposite shore, unless they could beach the craft and walk.

Soon they could hear a faint roar on the wind, which signaled their next challenge.

In only a few moments it was obvious that they must make for shore or perish going over a substantial cataract, as the noise had deepened.

A few moments later the mist in the air gave an indication how close the waterfall was. As the mist thickened it stifled sound. They rounded a bend and in the near distance the river simply disappeared in front of a vista of forests and farms in the distance. They were high above the treetops which spread out from the bottom of the cliff.

The current sped up. Endell knew he had to act quickly but

there was no obvious place to try to beach the boat. He grabbed the ferryman's pole and pushed with all his might on the right side of the boat. They entered the last slight turn of the river which pushed them to the left bank, doubly so with Endell's efforts. Evelyn screamed but there was no voice to her fear.

And while it seemed hopeless Endell was not paralyzed. He pushed hard a few more times then grabbed a rope and fastened it to the boat. As the current swept them around the last bend they were pushed toward the high far bank. Branches hung over the river and Endell calmly looked for an open branch, eyeing the edge of the falls rapidly approaching in front of them. Those in the boat could see the edge approach, and could clearly see the canopy of forest from above, stretching for miles from the bottom of the cataract.

He looped the rope over a strong limb which reached out over the water and tied the other end to the boat itself stopping it short of the cataract's edge. Relief swept the boat, replaced with their new predicament, now tied to a tree, with the river raging around them.

The height of the fall was dizzying but Endell choose to look at his task at hand, and slowly shortened the rope and moved the boat away from the strongest part of the current. And then he jumped the loop of rope along the branch inch by inch until they were close enough to reach the shore and push the boat close with the pole.

He was exhausted from his gargantuan effort.

The ferryman warned him that the water could still have an effect on Evelyn, but he refused to speculate what that effect might be. He explained he had seen people affected by the water and it was rarely the same outcome.

"The enchantments can be deep or light," he said. "And so far at least the maiden shows no obvious signs of evil. But do not let up your guard, she could show the signs at any time and with a rapid onset to become anything, from strangely aggressive to a mindless wraith."

127

"You seem too well acquainted with enchantments," said Endell with an edge. "Who is your lord and why have you been sent as ferryman to such a fiendish place?"

The ferryman dropped his head to his chest. It was a story he did not like to tell, but he felt compelled to speak with honesty at the request of this brave man.

"I am of noble blood and was engaged to marry the King's daughter. She was beautiful and his only child, therefore heir to his kingdom. The King had favored me, but a terrible accident at the ferry destroyed his faith in me.

"I was travelling with her and we approached this River Mead, much swollen with rain. I did not know about its secret. I did not know to fear its power and to take extra care. The surface was calm like it was today, but a huge wave singled her out and swept her away.

"I dove in to save her without any fear."

The ferryman described his courtship. His humbleness at meeting the King on other business and being introduced to his daughter, who was stately, calm and had a presence that he could not but notice.

"I loved her from the first time she spoke, or in truth, knew I could love her, as she seemed to float around me, with a grace I had never seen. In her, I could see my life unfolding into the future, every little thing. Her voice cast its spell on me and just laid bare my every thought.

"She was like those things you treasure from afar, those things you know their worth and want to get close to, knowing you can never actually possess them. No matter how close you get they are always separate, distinct and you cannot make it entirely part of you, like your thoughts are, your heart is, or the things you touch or see, no matter how clear.

"And so I was as near to her as one can be but it was my fate to lose her to the river wave, and, touching the water myself I was condemned to grow older but never to show my age. The King in his wrath assigned me to the river to keep my horror of his loss with me every day, and to remain young so I would always feel the loss deeply.

The ferryman told how others had rescued him from the water. He was enchanted and in a deep trance before they realized what had befallen him, his condemnation of eternal youth at a distance from life.

"The Lady Anne, the King's daughter was never found. And I must take a sip of river water daily or I slip back into a trance of the walking dead. I cannot go far from the water and so I became the ferryman."

"And every day I weep for my lady, lost in the very water I guard," as he spoke his eyes grew moist and his tears welled, making his countenance distant, like he was looking into the far future and past as the same moment in time.

They all sat quiet as the story ended. The Ferryman shook with a chill and told the group that they were within his King's boundaries and they should present themselves to him rather than be caught in the kingdom without his leave. For his part the King would ask for news from beyond his borders.

They had no choice but to make their way back several miles to the river crossing. They carried the small boat, stopping frequently to rest or pulled it along where the river bank was open enough to allow it. At the crossing Endell and Evelyn left the Ferryman in search of the King. Garland seemed anxious to move on land again but Evelyn privately feared the trailing evil - thinking it capable of following them across the river.

As they moved along the road they soon were confronted by two horsemen astride war horses and outfitted in royal livery with helmets and swords. They blocked the road and signaled Garland and Endell to stop.

"Well, a smelly farmer. What other faults do you have?"

"Faults. What has happened? I only seek the King to gain his leave to travel in these lands as I seek my fortune."

"Did you pass the ford?"

"The river was rough but we got across well down the stream. I can tell you the full tale but it isn't terribly interesting."

"Were you with the ferryman?"

"Yes, and we returned him to the ford to set things right. He told us to follow this road for about three days to find the King, though he did warn us of its dangers."

"Times have changed since he came this way. The kingdom is more powerful and the road quite safe, except for one evil fellow we cannot capture. He is quite powerful and despite our efforts he has remained at large among the peaceful lands, unmolested and our only blight."

They released Endell and his party to travel to the King but warned them to beware of the dangerous man and the King himself who was prone to unpredictability after the loss of his only child, a daughter. Not for the first time was this the fate of the royal house.

The road turned them west but twisted around so only the angle of the sun suggested their true direction. Pretty soon the country changed and they walked toward the blazing gem of a setting sun, with tilled fields on both sides and the forest edges all around. Endell realized that this place had been carved out of the heart of the forest.

Soon the peace was obvious as they passed a few inns and public houses where farm folk met and talked and where armies and soldiers existed only in stories. In the distance they could see the fabled castle, high on a rise. They heard tell of the King's golden throne and the peace of the realm. Evelyn seemed calmer, no longer on edge as the weight of the peace squeezed out thoughts of evil and fear.

As they neared the castle people were thick, the town spilling along the road. They entered a broad valley carved by the wide, slow river Orvalee, with the King's castle rising above it on a promontory rock. The castle was protected with high walls which reached down to the riverside to protect the port. As the sun went down the glow caught the honeyed walls and they shone a golden spark.

Endell wondered what this all looked like in bright light. Did the warm glow remain?

They seemed out of danger as they traversed the busy road but the valley took them with every step closer to Silas, the highwayman, hidden atop his horse in the warren of trees, fields, buildings and civilization.

Silas was huge and strong but always chose his victims from the weak and timid. He was cruel and would steal what he could and then beat his victims, inflicting fear and wounds upon them, because he could. They would not fight back for fear of worse. The King had a bounty on his head but they could not trap him.

As Endell rode toward a bridge in the valley, he could see, some distance in front of him, a boy riding a vegetable cart being pulled by an old horse. As the boy started across the bridge, a huge man came out of the trees and confronted the boy, blocking the road.

The boy knew he was in trouble. This was Silas the Highwayman, as near a monster as a human being. A giant of a man on a giant warhorse. His reputation usually led to his victims fleeing and surrendering their goods. The boy knew he could not fight such a monster as he would surely lose and maybe worse. And running would end with him caught and robbed, and a beating as bad or worse than if he confronted the highwayman directly.

But the boy, a 14 year old named Rodney, had thought long and hard about what he would do if he had the misfortune to be confronted by the scourge of Silas.

"Do not hurt me when you steal my vegetables, Sir Knight, because then I will be forced to fight for revenge. It is a curse I carry."

And Silas the robber laughed at him. "You think you can scare me with such talk? If I crush you in the face of such a claim, my reputation only grows, save among them who think your claim is nonsense."

He reined his horse and it reared up on its hind legs, towering above the boy and his cart.

"Such lies will be paid for," Silas anger rose. "Prepare to die. I would not want to be hounded by your curse and the quest for revenge should I let you live."

Silas unsheathed his sword and charged the boy. Rodney was not expecting such a turn of logic and leaped behind his cart using it as a shield, annoying the giant highwayman further. Silas' first swing missed wildly.

The boy challenged him with the only weapon he had, shaking his fist. Silas decided to end the charade and quickly dispense with this gnat of trouble.

Silas harbored a touch of concern in the deepest part of his brain, not liking to battle prophesy or magic. So he took an aggressive stance astride his steed and wielded his sword. He spurred the horse which leaped forward to smother the boy but Rodney twisted away and leaped over the containment wall of the bridge.

A broad flood plain was under the bridge with the river only a small portion of its spring strength. The leap took the boy to a bank of grass below the bridge.

Silas was furious that this mere child had eluded him. He could have taken the abandoned cart and been done with his robbery but he ignored the unguarded cart, dismounted his horse and went off the bridge and down the bank to find his quarry.

The boy had found a little cave, a hovel cut out of the bank by high water, and its entrance protected by tall grass. Out of the highwayman's sight, he figured he would be robbed and then could pick up the pieces after the highwayman had left. If Silas came after him, he was backed into a spot from which there was no escape. He did not understand the highwayman's determination to never be upstaged.

"Come boy," cooed Silas to himself, "where did you get to?"

At this time, Endell and his group had reached the bridge

and had seen the confrontation from afar. They knew the meaning of the vegetable cart all alone on the bridge, still tied to the horse pulling it. Silas' huge steed eyed them balefully. Garland sneered at the horse, the accomplice and bearer of evil.

Endell looked about him and saw a large man down on the bank below the bridge trampling the grass and stone, searching while talking to himself as he rooted about.

"Sir, does this pony and cart belong to you," Endell yelled down to catch the man's attention. "Will you sell me some food for my group is hungry?"

The large man merely looked up at him, unsure what to say. But a small voice from nowhere chimed up, "It's my cart. This large man is trying to kill me and steal it."

Endell was bemused.

"Is this true? And who's voice is making such a charge?"

The boy popped out of the long grass some distance away from Silas who was spoiling for a fight. The large man charged at him.

The boy ducked the blow and demanded the highwayman cease the fight.

Endell demanded he stop and explain why he had such violent intentions towards the boy.

"Has he wronged you? Why does this have to end in blood?"

Silas looked at Endell incredulous, "Sir, you are not armed. Be gone, you have no authority here nor any means to impose your will."

Silas turned back to his terrible task, attacking now without subtlety.

Endell leapt from Garland, angry at this vicious violence on a victim so young. He grabbed the vegetables from the cart and began to throw them at the giant. The boy did the same from the other side of him, with rocks collected from the river's edge.

As Endell pummeled Silas with raw vegetables, the boy, Rodney circled around Silas and got on the cart, moving it across the bridge to escape.

Evelyn gave the wooden lance to Endell but it was a weak weapon as Silas sported steel.

It was heavy and would not be easily break but Endell rightly feared a strong sword stroke against it.

Silas had moved back to reclaim his mount, coming off the river bank and onto the bridge. Endell was on foot. Silas charged. Endell, with the only choice available to him, stood in a crouch in the path of the Silas spear. Silas moved quickly to close the gap. Endell could see the horse's fury in his eyes and with his breath.

Closer and closer they came until they were upon Endell who dove across the horse's path while holding the lance parallel to the ground.

The dive got him out of the way of Silas' blow but put him under the horse's hooves. However the lance caused the steed to trip and sent him and his rider flying uncontrolled into a heap as they crashed onto the bridge.

Silas and his horse were dazed by the fall and its sudden and unexpected nature. Both rose slowly, shaking off the fall. Endell stood unhurt and looked at his lance, surprised it was still intact.

"Such strength should not exist in wood. This lance has a magic. Does it come from my defensive posture, my faith in it, or the purity of my intensions? I cannot say."

Evelyn marveled as well but was not as moved by the wood as she was by Endell's courage.

"I don't know if the lance is at the heart of this. But I triumphed in a battle with little hope. I name this lance 'Endurendil' and pray it sustains me through darkest battle as long as my virtue and vigor side with justice."

Silas struggled to his feet and found his sword.

"You are no farmer by light of day. You are a King's champion in disguise of gray. Doubtless there is a price on my head, as the King prefers his taxes to rob his subjects rather than my more direct approach. I have to set the matter straight, brave sir and you must die."

Silas gathered his shield and sword and moved to challenge Endell, who only had his staff and wits.

Silas approached and Endell waved to Garland to move away from the fray with Evelyn. The horse and rider moved toward the boy, Rodney who with his cart was now across the bridge and into the proper part of the town.

Endell readied his lance and saw that Silas mount displayed no pain or evidence of his fall. Endell parried Silas first stroke with Endurendil, though it bit into the wood. Before Silas could pull the sword free Endell pivoted and used the length of the lance to smash Silas in the head, knocking him off his steed and senseless.

Silas rolled to his feet and swore at himself for underestimating his foe a second time.

"Do not be aggressive without a plan," he muttered to himself. "Think and use your training and reflexes to parry the fight from this foe."

Endell knew his only chance was a mistake from Silas and so he taunted him trying to draw him into anger.

"You might beat a weakling, or a woman or a dwarf. Oh no, I forgot the boy bested you."

Silas clenched his muscles, unwilling to be drawn into the fight but Endell kept up the patter.

"You are awkward at best and have no style nor grace when you fight. And me, with no training, just a simple man garbed in gray, appears a fantastic fighter beside you."

Silas could not hold back his anger and swung at the slurs. And though his sword was quick Endell managed to turn aside the blows aimed at a quick and violent end to the battle.

Endell kept at it and Silas could not restrain himself from vicious blows that often did not connect at all. After many such blows Endell could see his foe was wearying. Silas took on the visage of one who knew he needed a quick end to battle or his hope for victory would fade with his loss of strength.

Endell knew instinctively that Silas was now at his most dangerous, as he wanted to end the fight quickly. Silas could slink away to fight again, but it was not his nature, so all that remained was to attack with all his remaining strength to end the battle once and for all time. He thought his reputation was already besmirched, with a victory now being the only way to stop the villagers from losing their fear of him.

Silas smashed blow after blow, at first parried by Endell, but the fury of the blows was such that Endell was forced down and pushed back onto one knee, with blood from smashed fingers flowing down his arms to his head and neck.

To observers Endell was being beaten down. But to Silas he could not finish the task.

Endell too was giving way hit by hit. Silas sensed he was nearly overcome, his opponent's strength spent. As soon as the lance was broken or cast aside, Endell would be defenseless and would be quickly overcome. Silas stopped trying to get his blows through to Endell and was content to chip away at the lance.

As Endell was battered down, down, Rodney ran to his cart and rooted amongst the vegetables searching for a weapon, a shovel, a hoe, but he found none as the giant pushed Endell to the edge of his defense, raging over him.

Endell blocked each blow without a thought as they rained down on him so fast they denied him a chance to fight back. His seeming ease of defense angered the giant and his mind began to wander to details, curiosities and movements of battle and changes that Silas might attempt. Endell thought of the end of the fight, when he would no longer be aware of his fate.

As these things rambled through his mind he stopped thinking of his parries. In his distraction a sword blow took off one of his fingers, causing blood to flow, but remarkably little pain.

However, the loss of his little finger on his left hand brought him back to the fight, sharpened his resolve and reinforced its determination that only one of the fighters would remain. It was too soon for his story to end thought Endell, as he considered taking an offensive swing.

And then an apple struck Silas in the head. The strangeness of this event cast a dreamlike quality over the battle.

The dream was broken when Rodney unleashed a stream of fruit upon the giant. Endell recognized his chance. He dropped the lance from one hand, acting as if he was no longer able to hold it. Despite the flying fruit which continued to annoy Silas the highwayman raised his sword up for a killing blow to the now defenseless Endell. That flourish gave Endell the needed seconds to swing the lance around like a javelin and thrust it with all his effort into the chest of the larger man. Silas sword swung wild.

Endell, now on both knees, collapsed forward with the blow, as the final sword swung missed him. He was spent. Silas spun with the sword stroke, as death took him before he could complete it. He turned and fell. Evelyn removed Endell from the battle scene and began to tend his injuries, wrapping his left hand to staunch the flow of blood.

News of the death of Silas quickly ran up the hill to the castle reaching the King. He sent a messenger requesting Endell to attend on him.

Though he could not walk, Endell was carried to the king. Upon seeing that Endell had vanquished Silas with only a wooden lance he granted Endell a kingly sword and shield and named him a Marshall of the Kingdom.

Taking water and some sustenance Endell was revived and

stood before the King.

"And we bestow upon you a chest of gold and lands of your own for defeating our long standing enemy. Our kingdom can sleep more soundly now knowing Silas is dead and soon to be buried."

Endell was humbled for a moment by the words of the King, thanking him for the gifts and rewards, but saying he really wanted the King's leave to root out other dangers to the realm. "Dangers that threaten the well off as well as the simple folk, farmers, tradesmen and every soul throughout the land."

"Fair said," enthused the King, "I grant you that wish. So fair is it to my ears that I insist you take the empty Castle Gremquest as your seat."

Endell was surprised at this bequest but was determined to use it well, telling the King that having such a fortress would aid his efforts, but that he would not back down from them.

"And yet, I will not live at Gremquest until I have completed my next tasks, such as you assign me. Once my name leads the lists of lore of this realm, I will claim your bequest."

And Endell asked for an exhaustive list of all the problems and deviltry known throughout the kingdom or that threatening it from just beyond its borders.

"Silas was our scourge, now defeated. I know only of rumors of other ruffians and evil doers. Check these and dispatch them as necessary and I will consider your vow paid."

Endell promised to wander to the borders and take control of them, north, south, east and west. He promised peace in the land and a quest to understand what drives these people to evil deeds.

"The virtuous deserve our defense of them and the evil doers deserve no mercy."

And Endell told the boy Rodney to take his family to Gremquest and make it operational and organized until such time as he could claim it fully.

"You and your family shall be the castellans and you shall carry the title Seneschal of Gremquest."

"But Sir Endell you will need a squire to assist you in your quests when you leave the castle and dwell in danger."

"Aye, I will require such a person but I can offer no training. Where might I find such an assistant who is fit and willing to face danger and have blood spilled?"

Endell lifted his gaze and looked about the gathering at the King's feet. A few caught his gaze but no one spoke up. But Rodney could not stay silent and spluttered as he tried to organize his thoughts to present himself as a possible squire.

Endell couldn't hold his steely gaze and dramatic temperament. He began to crumble in mirth.

"Yes, Rod you shall be my squire, if that is your desire. Our first task is to travel with Evelyn to resolve her situation. In doing so we may find other problems to deal with."

Endell enquired after the Castle, wanting to know its history and what fate rendered it empty and forlorn.

One of the King's attendants spoke up explaining that Gremquest was near the ferry where a noble family lived for generations until fate crossed a young heir's path and the tragedy that ensued destroyed him, and the King's wrath of old ended the family title. A title which has been void for many centuries.

"King's justice comes from God, inspired and handed down, it is not ours to question. Such justice comes from the sum of all needs, deterrence, justice, the needs of the kingdom, penalties of law and retribution. Should common men, with no background or authority stand in judgment of those who beg forgiveness or claim their innocence? How would men accept justice dispensed that was not divinely inspired?"

Endell wondered aloud if this tale of the Castle was a myth, a fantasy formed over the lengthy time since it occurred. He wanted to know if the Castle still stood strong.

"Be the walls sealed and strong? Who knows as dust will cover all things. No one has been inside the walls in many a life of man. And now the King sees fit to bestow it on you. The people near it will welcome the castle come back to life and trust the justice that comes from it."

"Legends say that the fortress holds are huge with passages and rooms that confuse and perhaps hold treasures still, fine art, maps and a library of knowledge. The Castle has a reputation for magic and ghosts and spirits who converse with long dead lords on many subjects from money and taxation to the doings of men."

The speaker did acknowledge that such stories were merely stories embellished and retold in local pubs and as bed time stories for children, as no one had entered the Castle for many years.

So Endell took his leave of the King and gathered his party and those that would join him to make for Gremquest, and take charge of the ancient works of stone.

Provisioned and ready the small party set out from the King's Castle Orvalee but not before the King himself saw them off and provided to Endell a great key to open the gate.

"Castle Gremquest is your fee for ridding us of Silas the terrible, thief and scourge. I beg an annual tribute of a single red rose from you to acknowledge me as your liege lord, no, make it a red and white rose in alternative years. It is but a small acknowledgement."

Endell knelt on one knee and bowed his head to the King.

"And thus it shall be my great and noble King. Each year I will deliver a fragrant rose and hand it to you as part of my report about doings on our hinterlands. And now I ride to Gremquest."

The King waved him on and Endell waved back his four fingered hand. The party rode leagues each day taking a wide route to learn about the Kingdom. They encountered little adventure though Endell's fame and task preceded him. The group rode together at leisure having time to speak to one another.

"This has been very hard on me, dear Endell," said Evelyn. Endell knew she was not poking fun for since she sank in the river she had spent much of her time and attention on Endell who saved her. She also talked a great deal about the ferryman's situation.

Endell wondered if her obsessions would be blunted if she touched the water or took a daily sip as the ferryman had to do. For the ferryman needed it or he would lose consciousness and perhaps die, while Evelyn merely seemed strangely preoccupied with the incident. He wondered if there was anything he could do, and decided to himself that additional contact with the river water might have consequences worse than her current plight.

"Magic, Rodney, is a terrible thing." And the boy looked at him for more. "There is no consistency, and study has revealed little detail to necromancers or magicians who try to understand it."

"So stay away, I say. Have nothing to do with it."

"Wise words boy, wise words. I know nothing of the grip this magic has on Evelyn." And they walked in tandem with Garland setting the pace. "We will avoid it as we can but sometimes it does not avoid us."

Endell knew that no magic may be in play, given Evelyn's predilections, but still he worried and had grown protective of her. On her part she seemed much closer to Endell, but he put that to his defense of her and willingness to do battle on her behalf. He did not speculate further.

They no longer seemed to be pursued by evil, though they had left the forest cover behind. Endell wondered if the spell she faced was voided in the Kingdom, even if the Kingdom was surrounded by the Wood. Still she had grown emotional about him and he couldn't help but wonder if it was the work of the river water.

If he wanted a wife she was suited, beautiful with regal bearing, youthful and blond. She seemed willing and even excited when he asked for her hand.

"You have read my mind. I have waited on you, for this I feel was fated since we met. We have much to do to prepare."

Evelyn said the curse under which she lived must be removed before they could be united, she did not want that looming over them in the future. She told Endell that with her curse still in place he would not be fully able to conduct his promises to the King as he would be worried for her. And if the price was her life then it was better knowing that than having a touch only, of hope for release.

Endell said that he believed the problems she faced stemmed from one thing and to fix that would remove all the attendant evil that pursued her.

"Silas was the only known enemy of this land but once we arrived there have been reports of evil doings all around the borders. I believe you have been followed here, and the evil that is drawn to you is gathering in strength and surrounding us. It appears to me that this kingdom is really just carved out of the Garadreium Wood, the forest of the world that contains all."

Endell was determined to leave so that evil would stay away from the kingdom. He did not want to be responsible for mayhem that may be visited upon the town's folk. He would face it on his terms on another field of battle.

"Rod, which way should we go to escape the Wood?"

"You think the Wood ends somewhere? It is magic incarnate, the natural state of the world, presided over by the Faery Queen. I know of no end or edge though there are some enclaves like the present kingdom which are carved out of the trees. I cannot guide you."

And so Endell believed his only hope was to venture forth, to follow the trails through the Wood and find his fate, even if he was walking into certain battle. He knew that either way, such a battle would determine his fate.

As they neared the Castle Gremquest, Endell spoke.

"There is the castle black and tall. It must be reclaimed from the elements and set to order. Ward, father of my squire, on you I charge this task, be the Seneschal of the Tower, forever. I go to seek evil that may befall the kingdom, I would like to know that I may return to a functioning home. But the challenge to make it so, is yours and the glory in success will be yours also. I hope to return successful in my tasks, honor intact, to doors that open for me."

Ward and his company departed to the Castle though some wanted to ride with Endell to whatever glory might come. Endell waved them off, saying a small, nimble group was best. Others were content to do the castle work that would make Endell happy if he returned.

The three valiant seekers were left. They considered the road. They considered the trees. They watched their companions ride for Gremquest.

And then Endell signaled Garland to move into the Wood, headlong without fear. After the edge was conquered their footfalls ceased to sound, silence gave away nothing as they moved past the flora of the forest, oak trees, tall and sturdy, beech trees slender and light. They passed bushes and flowers, moved around of through brambles and roots. The minutes turned to hours as they had no road nor even a rough path.

Their progress was painful, slow, and their hope for a quick confrontation and resolution of the evil pursuit was hollow in their minds. And yet they kept at it, in silence, without complaint, moving forward through the disorganized land hoping to find a path be it straight or crooked.

And slowly the air itself grew thick, blackness encompassed them so slowly they did not perceive it. The evil intentions billowed, grew and seemed deep and so wide there was no penetration for relief or escape.

The tension rose for all in the company but most with Evelyn on whom it was focused.

"Stop this dream," she cried in torment, reigning her horse and looking about wildly for a source of the pressure.

And then mildly she spoke, "Take me! The curse has won. I thought I was free of it, but alas only a little while. The devils have won a victory over love and shall be greater and emboldened by their success. The demons are come."

Rod on his mount stared with wide eyes at Evelyn and her outburst.

Endell guessed that the evil that pursued her had made itself known to her, she could see it and feel its power. She was helpless to its bidding and hopeless in its presence.

For she sat still, fear in her eyes, gazing into the very jaws of hell.

Endell reared Garland on his hind legs and leapt to her. She was nearly encompassed by evil but he managed to place himself between it and it's victim, moving between the abyss and her, in challenge to it. And that broke the spell, the darkness, which had been deepening, fell away and Rodney, who had lost sight of her, now witnessed her emerging from the black and back into the daylight.

"Never give in to anything evil and pay no heed save escape unless you decide to kill it. It is a malignant parasite feeding on your honest desire to believe that your wish for the betterment of others is a selfless hope. We have hope in abundance and goals to fulfill. We shall make for open skies, and if challenged we will do battle and either live or die."

And they moved forward and up a small bank and onto a road stretching out into the distance in both directions.

"Now we have a chance, direction, space to fight."

The path was a fair road, graded and smooth to hoof or cart. But on closer inspection it turned away and did not go straight in either direction as it avoided boulders, trees and whatever else lurked in the Wood that was necessary to avoid.

"I would so like the road to be straight, so our intentions were obvious. Not knowing our destination causes pain and worry," said Rodney.

"Follow me, we cannot rest, though we weary be. I expect around some turn we will find what we are looking for. We do not flee. Yes Rod, I am afraid too, but not for me but for my love for Evelyn and my responsibility to you. Unless we are fated to a future, we will die here, even if it is a death in celebration of our desire to succeed and make our lives much more.

They rounded a corner and saw another in the distance, with the pressure mounting on their expectations. But they did not despair, rather they laughed at the folly of it all, as they picked their way along the path to face their destiny only to have it stretch out again.

Around another corner and then they saw it. A straight road with a glimpse of salvation, a bright white light, shining out along the road framed by trees and a leaden, low sky.

They broke into a gallop, seeing the safety of their future, trying to reach it. But the road seemed infinite, they drew no closer. As they slowed they realized they had to face their fears, just as huge evil monsters came from the wood and blocked the road.

Three giants, crouched across the road, identical in motion, with an evil intent that was in their countenance.

Endell continued his approach, raising Endurendil, his mighty lance, before him, signaling he was prepared to fight.

Evelyn saw the surrounding woods were filled with fell creatures, evil, blocking their escape. These creatures seemed to have emerged from the very earth, as they were covered in dirt and slime, and they stank like the bowels of hell, brimstone, putrid flesh, and decay. Their black breath coated the air, the source of the black despair they had already experienced but now was close and real.

And Endell held Endurendil. It glowed a golden light, shining

145

brighter, a flare, a burst warding off the confidence of the evil multitude.

The golden light did not dim, but the triple horror did not back away from it. Endell kept his pace to break the giants bar to their progress. He trusted his golden lance and buried it in the center giant.

One of the huge fell creatures took a swing at him and missed, slashing Rodney's pony with his razor claws, and knocking the unfortunate pony out from underneath the doughty squire who had advance each step with Endell, pulled along in his wake, and unafraid.

Rod's pony stood shocked at the blow. It was still for a moment and then began to walk slowly away.

Soon whatever weapon the giant had hidden in his grip did its work as a line of blood followed the slash along the length of the stunned pony.

From a trickle of red along the line and fear in the pony's eyes, to a wide rent in its hide, from its neck to its back flank, the flesh rent wide open, and gushed the life blood. The pony fell, kneeling in a pool of its own blood, full red and changing as it pooled to a deeper color, now with a brownish hue.

Rodney was thrown from the animal, which looked at him dolefully, as it knew it could no longer fulfill its task and bear him.

The pony died with its virtue obvious to all, as it never backed down nor tried to run from fear. The animal shed a tear and Rodney did too.

And as Rodney expected another killing blow, then a light shone, and the sky lifted its darkness. A panorama of well tilled fields, of homes and civilization spilled out around him.

He whacked himself in the temple unable to believe what he saw. And then there was a hand on his shoulder, and Endell looked down at him with joy.

"That evil projected an endless path to enhance the hopelessness we were to face. Once we ran through the spell and past the edge of the forest we met the fell giant. It projected itself in three to triple our fear."

The giant had succumbed to the killing thrust of Endurendil, and the curse lifted.

"Your faithful pony blocked the giant's sweeping blow and provided the opening for my thrust."

Using a shaky finger, as she was not fully convinced the curse had been foiled, Evelyn pointed back at the wood directly behind them, where they saw hundreds of pairs of eyes, forms of evil in the shadow of the forest.

"Be gone yon hellions, the curse is thrown down, you have no business with us," Endell commanded.

And with that they all began to melt. Hissing and melting into a black mist which rose through the trees and met the wind above the canopy. And there the mist was blown away, and nothing remained of their horror save the memory.

Endell had defended the kingdom by himself with Evelyn and Rodney along for the task.

"The curse is struck down and follows us no more. We can proceed with our lives and add to our list of adventures."

"Oh yes, dear Evelyn and stout Rodney, all the king's subjects will bleat their praise for us saving their common lives. For they are afraid of taking it on, of facing their fears. None of them aspire as I do, to be someone, to do uncommon things, to explore the depths and the heights, to breathe in valleys and mountains and see the entire world as my own ground. I will roam the unknown and battle my way up from obscurity to renown."

"You are noble Endell my dear, but do not lose your humbleness of tone and approach," said Evelyn.

"Fight for the common man, as they have taken on common tasks but no less important to the operation of the world.

They live simply and you can earn their admiration and rise above them, a hero. But remember, the rabble decide the duration of your elevation. Treat them well and remember despite your honest actions you are not immune from temptation and evil. We all need to trust in the fate assigned to us which rules us, dust to dust."

End Part One

Part Two - The End of Evil

Wandering near his Castle home Endell, the new lord of Gremquest, chanced upon a newly bloomed flower, and he marveled at the intoxicating scent it produced.

Without the aroma he might have missed the flower, despite its pure white petals and long, deep green stem which lifted it out of the general ramble of undergrowth.

In fact, the plants around it seemed to part for its growth, giving it space to rise. And the scent was a fragrance so lovely that people hunted the flower and made songs of its splendor.

He found upon enquiry that it was called Avowan by those horticulturalists who prized it above all others, for the perfume could be distilled and had powerful effects. It was difficult to grow and seemed to thrive in the wild only in specific places, where once established it would reappear each year. Horticulturalists would drop their cultivation of lilies or fine orchids if there was a sighting.

Unaware of all of this, Endell gently dug one out still in the earth in which it had grown and brought it inside the Castle where it could flourish in sanctuary. It was to be the emblem of his lady, Evelyn, and he presented it to her as he formally asked for her hand.

They had already discussed the possibility but had foresworn the day until their fears and evils had been laid to rest. Evelyn, intoxicated or not from the water of the enchanted river, was thrilled at Endell's desire and acceded to his wishes.

Gremquest was made ready for the ceremony. Everyone in the Castle and surrounding lands were invited to the feast.

Locals were at first surprised the castle was being reclaimed and happy as they saw it steadily improved and made ready. Broken masonry was repaired, the portcullis was improved and the castle itself made for inhabitants again. The flower

Avowan was used to decorate the castle walls and ways, in paintings, and woven into tapestries which adorned the inside stone walls of passageways and even specific chambers.

The flower seemed to lift everyone's spirits. Endell made it the central figure on his banner which he flew over the castle from the highest tower. He crossed the stem at an angle with the stave of Endurendil, featuring the notch that Silas had inflicted upon it, and a smear of red for the blood that was shed.

And on his shield a single Avowan was laid over a silver background, with a swath of gold which produced a striking pennant, shield and sigil of his house.

When the pennant was first revealed it brought much happiness to those who saw it, as the castle had come back to life with a champion its owner, one who might someday attract the king to these local lands.

The story of Endell was known to all, with embellishments and extra details added in the retellings which added luster to his heroism. At the heart of it, he was brave and bold beyond reason. And there was no disavowal of those details by Endell, and no discord among those who lived in the area.

As they were preparing the Castle the sun rose each day with new orders coming for food and entertainment and local artisans to help return the castle to its glory and be ready for the feast.

After the ceremony Endell and Evelyn settled in to their lives. Peace reigned for years with plentiful rain for crops, and mild winters. But it could not last forever as Endell himself knew.

And at the outset of one particular winter, a storm brewed in the north and fell down on Gremquest, as snow fell like thick milk pushed by a demonic wind raging with ice and fear. Even the morning sun could not break through and the storm raged all day and into the next.

The next day Endell arose to silence. The storm was gone,

even if the sky still showed of storm clouds. There was no wind. Looking out from the battlements all anyone could see was a blanket of white with nothing to break it or give perspective. It even merged in the deep distance with the thudding sky disguising the true horizon.

Endell believed the storm was not natural. Stories circulated in the castle suggesting the storm had buried farms entirely. Many such places had no defense against the power and suddenness of attack, especially as their buildings lay low slung and spread out across the land.

Endell called for Rodney his seneschal for advice as the younger man was familiar with the lands and the expectations of the storm and the people who lived through it. However, Rodney was not in the castle when the storm hit.

A day, then another, and Endell grew concerned though he believed that Rodney must be stuck at a farm waiting to dig out and return to the castle knowing he would be called upon.

And as the reality of the storm lay heavy after the fall, and the third day slowly moved through the thin rays of early evening, the bleakness was broken by a single rider, strong of limb and countenance, pushing through the deep snow. He came without sigil nor identification for he needed none. He was Rodney grown from a boy into a man who Endell knew well. His horse, a powerful black stallion, struggled against the heavy white snow, forced to lift its legs high to lessen the weight of the stuff. It was obvious to anyone watching that the horse had long ago settled into a stride, slow but continuous through the white powder. How long they had been churning together against the white powder no one knew.

Though only a few years older than when he rode his vegetable cart he had been that age when most change happens to a young man, and so had grown into an adult.

For time itself can make but half a man, the rest comes from his courage, his deeds and his reaction to those things that occur to him and around him. This struggle was one of those things, though he did not think of it as such.

And while there is universality in this growth, not all experience it and few do, in exactly the same way. Some children can display this bravery and breed it to a high pitch. And many an old codger has never stood and faced down his enemy or his fear.

Rodney reached the castle gate and entered, finally free from the hold of the snow.

"This blanket of snow is foul and must go," said Endell. "I think some evil has caused this snow to put us to fear, to soften us for more plagues, to wall us in from one another. I will go forth and face it alone if that's what it takes."

"Two things are amiss with that plan," said Rodney. "First, I shall go with you regardless and have your back as you seek out a foe. And second you need a plan for finding this evil, a quest to root it out."

As Rodney made clear all quests have a goal, but this one seemed ill-defined beyond hope for success. And while Rodney feared no evil he did not desire a life roaming the land looking for trouble but never finding it, looking for something that they did not even define.

"Yes, you are right Rodney, my desire to end this soared beyond calibration of a goal. We need an objective. I think a trip to the legendary Mithomere and a gaze into its oracle depths may provide a path for our quest."

And with Rodney's nod in support of his idea, Endell's spirits were raised and the two planned to ride to seek deliverance from the blanket of white.

"We must ready the horses, ready the castle for our departure. I will ride Garland into the fearsome Garadreium Wood but there I have already stood and faced fears twenty fold that of mere wind and snow and biting cold."

He prepared to tell Evelyn of his need to go, summoning a servant to fetch her to him.

As he explained, she knew he must go, as his supporters and surrounding land owners demanded it of him as the price he paid to be the master of the Castle. He told her that he knew not how long he would be away as he first had to seek out whatever was causing the spell of winter before he could advance upon it.

Evelyn understood and was comforted that Garland would carry him, for she had come to love the horse and believed it a source of strength for her husband.

"I shall live in fear for you until you return," she said. She gave him a chain of gold with a token to wear around his neck while he was gone.

Endell kissed her brow and swept her long hair back from her face, and smiled softly at her love, and his shone through.

"I have no fear," he said, except for you, should we not be able to return our lands to their natural state. I am of the mind that magic of some kind has created this snowy cover."

He looked down at the pendant on the chain and saw an enameled Avowan, perfect and flawless, and he laughed in mirth.

"A laugh is the best cure for solemn times and solemn speech. I may be away a time but vow to return with the quest fulfilled and the land repaired."

The morning dawned blue and clear and cold. Endell and Rodney issued from the castle gates accompanied by a few squires and men at arms. It was a party large enough to brave the quest and small enough to do it with speed.

Rodney's mount, the steed Vega, was black against the snow with a hint of a lighter hue of deep blue on its chest and hinds where its legs met its body, and the hint of a patch on its forehead.

A crowd had gathered at the portcullis gate to see them off.

"Fear not as I have no fear," Endell called out to the gathering.

"Faith will not fall, though I may return bloodied, I will return."

With those words he turned Garland in silence and walked slowly from Gremquest in search of his immediate destiny and a solution to the biting cold. And while they walked from the Castle with their heads held high, the bright sunshine warming the air, it wasn't long before their heads had shrunken down between their shoulders and scarves swathed their heads and faces, as the sun weakened and the cold nipped with a sting.

Several days later they had seen hints of others about, footprints in the snow, even a line of men gone to battle, but to where, the rumors and tracks told nothing. The snow cover did become thin as they went, leading Endell to believe it was Gremquest that was the target of some wrathful evil. And as they reached the forest eves the snow was no more, save when they looked behind them from whence they had come and it was a blanket still without break in perspective.

"The Kingdom is an island in the Wood, and island of snow, as I would guess the whole of our lord's kingdom was blighted, and the evidence of fighting men from the king is what we saw crossing our path. I should like the King to know we have taken action."

There was talk that perhaps the King had sent for them, and a few of the men wondered if they should turn back, but Endell would have none of that talk. Rodney said that he was sure the King would receive word of their quest. But in the end Endell sent back a single rider to inform the King of their plan, and let him know they were addressing the problem.

And while the forest for its faults in harboring evil, seemed more fair, without snow and with sunshine, there was no birdsong, no forest beasts on the roam. Endell wondered aloud what had chased them away.

And a quiet voice answered his query.

"T'was fear of the cold. Most beasts were unprepared for it and fled and the other half fled for their loved ones, afraid of the cold on their behalf."

The voice was all around them and they looked hard at every hiding place but saw nothing.

"They've gone I said, far away from the pain of these places."

"Who art thou who speaks and still remains here so alone that he rules by proxy?"

"Oh, no king am I, though I have some skill in the art of science which I command to my will."

The voice became smaller and no longer surrounded them. But its power held the company to its mystery and compelled them to listen.

And then from behind a large tree, stepped an old man, ragged and stooped. The sun was behind him but blocked mostly by the forest welling up behind him. Sunbeams managed to poke through between the trees.

"Come," he waved, "these trees, this forest I know. Follow me." And he ambled into the forest toward a hill which created a hollow.

He walked straight into the sun though there was no path anyone could see. And yet there was a straight course, wide enough for horses to traverse with ease.

"I wonder who this wanderer is?" asked Rodney quietly beneath his breath and sword. "I sense strong magic in him and we needs be as cautious as we can."

"Fear not this wizard," said Endell in a commanding voice, "We will make him party to our counsels as he appears to be immune to the spell of cold and snow. His advice will be most welcome as we know so little."

And the company passed trees and found a sheltered dell beneath the hill they had seen. And in the dell stood a dwelling with a door made of seashells and other bits of hardened nature. Made stranger still as no ocean was known to the forest dwellers.

They entered and saw a fire burnt so low that their shadows outstripped it and leapt up the walls, like animals reaching for something, food or enemies, or a man reaching to heaven but not grasping what he seeks.

The room was strangely shaped and stuffed with books and herbs and sported a dust so thick it could not be disturbed. And it held a silence, brewing through many years and guarding something fearful and very secret. A corner held a small suit of armor, caked in dust and with so dull a shine that it was hardly noticed as they entered.

In nooks and corners, where what little light there was in the room illuminated various things, were contained many things, showing the old man had wide interests. There was one torch on the wall beside the fireplace. The man lifted it and applied it to the kindling in the fireplace.

A faint pattern played on the walls, leaping and diminishing as the flame flickered. It revealed each visitor's desire, by what they chose to focus upon, each in their turn riveted to the dance of flame.

"Please sit, my friends," beckoned the host who slid into a comfortable chair. "Find a spot and rest your legs and hearts and be rid of your aches and pains of a long journey."

The old man said they had time enough to talk and speak to all their questions. He promised to be forthcoming and speak of evil and good.

Endell looked upon the man fully engaged in every detail, from his speech to his dress to his mannerisms. Rodney however, shifted his attention seeing all manner of things and was unable to keep his eyes in any one place.

Having added wood and tending the fire, it rose and fell at times illuminating the room completely and other times looking as if it might leap from the fireplace and catch on papers or furniture or tapestries.

"This cold has come and magic cannot stop it. I have searched for the nature of this problem but found only that it is connected to a King Arrol. Endell started, he had heard that name before in some forgotten tale or story, but he could not place it.

In that short silence the flames slowly rose as the silence deepened. Endell remained unmoved, in thought and still shocked by the partly remembered detail.

"Is that person known to you? You appear to have some knowledge of that name."

And the fire settled back, now only glowing embers.

And Endell started to speak, without thinking, his lips moved and he told what he knew in a monotone of speech, that he had somewhere heard the evil name.

"Where did you hear this name?" Endell asked. "And what part does he play in the coming of the cold and snow?"

The old man told that he believed that finding this King would answer their questions and that time was important and should not be wasted thinking about their search and its reasons.

And Rodney chimed in declaiming that they should move quickly to find the Mithomere, and admitted to the old man that this had been their quest from the start of their journey. He added that the cold was far worse outside the wood and that people were suffering and might not survive if the freeze was not lifted quickly.

"You are rash, young Rodney, though among the young that is not odd. However, if you wish to live long and well you will have to take a more measured view of your tasks."

And the old man held up his hand to stop a response, claiming it of no value to their task. He begged them to leave and continue their quest to find the heart of evil. Thinking at first and then speaking out loud, Endell said that the old man's knowledge and magic might be of value and that he should join them. And as he said it, he started to believe it.

"I am not just a magician, I can command the wind and

speak with all living things. And I know the way in which you seek, a path to the Mithomere, I can guide you but you have to trust me, as with all the forest ways it will seem roundabout and unclear. Calamities and fear will follow us as we journey to the oracle water in search of the purity of prophesy by way of her young daughter. The oracle should reveal and cast light on the reality we seek, and help us tear back the darkness and cold which has the earth in its hands."

The wizard made those few preparations necessary to wizards and they left as speed was important to them. The wizard led the way and told fair and magic tales of lore as they journeyed. He told of princes play, knightly pranks and quiet vales of thought. And though he tried to say little of himself bits and pieces of his life were revealed to the company. He often spoke of Sebastian and the company suspected he was speaking of himself but when they put it to him, the wizard demurred saying his name was Herorot.

And another story emerged as Herorot told of his father, who was travelling the road which runs from the sea to the King's Castle and passed an inn called the Anchor and Crown. He heard warnings from the locals of a huge dragon like beast, wingless but fierce with a hide tempered and tough so that no blade or point could pierce it.

The wizard continued saying the worm had captured the inn and killed many men, strong and bold who had stood their ground in his face as he claimed the building and its contents. The beast also bested many others who came to reclaim the building and kill him.

"But my father was a fighting man from birth," Herorot said. "And he cared little for fair words, except in good times. So he took a swig of ale, wiped his lip, grabbed his sword and shield and took another sip. Then he marched full on into the inn, though silent, to face the horrific beast with his sword."

"No sound came from the Inn for many an hour and the people who watched grew chilled as they believed that the beast had killed again. The tension grew and grew until my father emerged with a large mug 'o mead at his lips.

"Enter" he told the crowd, "The beast is dead, though I'm not sure how as I struck no blow against it." And they all drank into the night upon whence my father left quietly, leaving my mother and me as a babe alone. And thence she gave me my name, and told the story to an old childless couple and gave me to them to raise. They were kindly but dead before a score of years had passed. I shed the first and last of my tears at that."

"But what of Sebastian who you spoke of at length? Is he real or just a fiction, a place to park your stories?" asked Rod.

And a faraway look glazed the wizard's eyes, reflecting a depth of knowledge and his soul where his emotions were held in many packages, each being examined many times, each facet of their reality never completely understood. It was evident that the wizard held some unfinished concern when it came to that name, as blame for whatever had befallen him was not yet assigned in full.

"He was my only son," said the wizard softly.

His eyes glazed at the memory and he shook his head and eyes hard to clear his mind. "But that was long ago and far away from here."

And he waved his hand at the far mountainous horizon and fanned away the memories as if they were a thick smoke surrounding him.

The fellowship remained silent, caught in the wizard's emotion and not wanting to upset him with further questions. And too, all save the magician, they shifted their thought to the land which had risen up as they walked through the forest and been unable to see it clearly. They emerged in a clearing and as the wizard waved at the horizon they all saw the mountains clearly, now filling their view. The cold and colors made it difficult to see where the mountains ended and the sky began. They continued on, though they were funneled into a valley between two arms of the mountains as it was much easier going. They journeyed deeper into this valley until they reached the mountain's roots and they were swallowed whole.

It was a cave, carved into a high stone wall, above which rose the mountain rising far above their ability to see it.

Darkness oozed from the cave, malevolent as if the very light itself had been extracted and the darkness reached out into the surrounding woodland, groping like a sightless hand, reaching, reaching like the tide on the strand. It stretched out as if trying to cover something it might find and pull it back into the cave.

As they got closer, reaching it from aside the blackness, they could see there were remnants of a door, once ornate that framed the yawning blackness and gave weight to the nameless fears which hide in every breast. They could all feel those fears push their hearts into their own ribs making it harder to breathe. The fears tingled their nerves and widened time as each moment was lengthened and multiplied without adding to it.

And Herorot spoke quite calmly, "Follow fearless." And everyone believed his strength and knew not that he was forcing his courage. He reached inside his cloak and found a jewel which bore a bright light upon his command. He held it high and spoke the words and the light burst forth casting back the black. And there revealed was no cave but a grassy plain with no ceiling save sky.

"What deviltry is this?" cried Endell whose hand had gone to his broach, the talisman he had been given for courage. And as he clutched it, all disappeared and a scream broke his thoughts and he turned to see Rodney striking the wall with his sword.

Again with a triumphal shout the sword smote the stone, biting into it, but there was no enemy there that anyone could see, though Rodney saw something to fight.

Evil dwelt there, giving Rod the illusion that there was something to attack. And Endell grasped that each of them

160

saw something different. He saw a wide plain and Rodney saw a figure to fight. Their squires stood still confused at the sights of their masters doing things which did not make sense. They wondered if their eyes lied to them and drew their weapons in defense. They were all rooted to their spots though no chains held them as their perceptions gave them reason for their action or lack of it.

"We must go," said Endell slowly without fear shading his words. "This great grassland is very wide it appears."

And Herorot agreed it was best to keep moving, but his speech was shaky and unsure as he couldn't really see the grassland clearly, though he perceived it was there.

"Away" yelled Endell's young squire, a command. And he leapt high and plunged his dagger into the dry ground. It was dry ground to all but him as black blood drenched his blade and a tentacle appeared to view, twitching in death in Endell's shade. Endell had not seen the danger and did not immediately understand the heroic act of his attendant.

Endell had left to move into the plain and Rodney followed into a crevasse in the stone, a cave, marveling at Endell's fearlessness with the dark way.

And Rodney saw his whole life with uncommon clearness before the present jolted back and all that was left was the memory of complete illumination which had come in total and without warning. It happened so fast and was so complete that he could not grasp any detail nor had any element of the perception except that he had had it.

Each mind of the travelers encountered the enigma of their own perception, but they perceived no flaw with the others and their journey. And that of course is the way all men move through their lives, acting upon their own perception of reality around them while they walk or crawl in the direction they perceive to be the best for them. Sane or insane it matters not, for each person's perception of reality is their own truth without exception.

And as they moved their perceptions did merge and their

confusion among each other fell away as the equal experience of walking brought their thoughts together, fueled by the excitement that danger was among them.

The five, Endell, Rodney and their two squires, joined with Herorot the wizard, and now faced a forest, dark, with each step they took echoing like it was the last and lonely and stark.

No sunlight reached this forest floor and no flower or color of any kind was in sight, only the drab green and brown of the forest floor and the trees, rotting wood and dead leaves which covered the floor like an unending funeral pall.

And Endell walked with purpose saying to any and all that they were near to their destination. The wizard was not so confident. And then with a shout, voices broke the empty land and Endell sprang towards the trouble with Rod hot in pursuit. The wizard stayed back and melted into the landscape finding a vantage point to observe. He decided that he would intervene only if things went badly against the company.

Endell burst past some trees which had not been there before, wielding Endurendil his lance while keeping his sword sheathed.

He begged Rod to follow and they jumped into a fight to help a lone warrior, who was surrounded by a dozen evil seeming, defiant attackers. Endell swung his great lance first and swept two of the attackers away. Their eyes remained burning fires of hell but aside they stood. They did not dissipate nor leave and they seemed to have lived every evil deed that has ever been.

They knew not joy or love only rage, tormented by the sights of those who were not demon seed, and thereby damned to remain forever fixed by the ghastly fires of hell. They could not close their eyes nor even blink.

Two were cast down by Endell, staring with red eyes, their view returned to the devil himself. The remaining 10 wraiths now turned on Endell freeing the lone warrior they had happened upon to attack in his turn.

He wielded a heavy metal chain of many links and it whistled as he swung it. He was deadly in its ways and down went five wraiths, their eyes turned to burning coals, flickering a ghastly red, deep in their evil spells. The remaining wraiths gathered their fell strength, seeming to gain the power of those who had been stopped, and so fought with a fury of the original 12.

But as a few more were bested they gave up the fight, vowing to return again.

The warrior dropped his chain, his hand had been burnt where he had grasped a link.

"My hand has never dealt so deadly a blow," he held it to soothe the pain. And a white mist rose as the chain disintegrated into the air and the smoke was blown away on the wind.

The threat ended, Endell asked the name of the chain warrior who had defended himself so ably.

"Kevin, is me, protector of . . . " he turned and looked about him. "She is gone. I am the protector of one who was not concerned about me or my valor."

He insisted that there was a lady to whom he swore his honor and in proof gave her his glove as a talisman, the same glove that was missing from his burned and injured hand, which he held out to their view to prove his speech.

"This princess bears a prize to her father and I must guard her to prove myself true," Kevin said. "But she goes fast and where and when she wants making my task terribly difficult. She has used this battle as cover for her escape, perhaps not trusting my prowess. But I am still here and the wraiths are no more, I have survived again and continue to battle."

And then a voice came down, 'twas Herorot almost singing a claim that his magic infused the chain, multiplying with magic the power of the knight in his claim to protect the girl.

"It is a power beyond love itself," he said.

"Beyond love? Such a power exists?" asked an incredulous Endell.

And Herorot nodded in vigor, explaining that he drew from his own life a love that rests on friendship rather than desire, as desire can trip those who experience it only, and in the end can cause great pain.

"It was me who charged the chain with white heat, enough to cripple the devil's horde."

And Endell turned to Kevin and asked him to join their quest and they would join his in turn. And Kevin bowed low and joined with them in pledge to undertake the mission of their house without need for them to reciprocate. Then Endell spoke, committing his party of five and their families to help Kevin in his quest with the maiden with everything they possessed.

"My troth is pledged and an oath I swear that I will save your life should it be necessary and help you find your wife to be."

And Endell laughed with such joy that the creatures of the glade awoke and ran hither and yon through the under-growth, past the trees and through the grasses paying no heed to the company or the time of day. Beasts ran, birds flew from the joyous noise, even insects swarmed the air despite the cold, but none of the company noticed the completeness of the rising life that Endell's laugh had sparked.

And Endell turned to Herorot the wizard and asked him to find the girl that Kevin had pledged to help, despite the whirlwind of events that had just transpired.

"Indeed I will find her, but I must counsel at the Mithomere, which I believe is very close to here."

And Kevin rose to protest but Herorot waved, "Quiet! Come I can hear the fountain. You knaves must trust me."

And they pushed through the wood and lo came the sound of falling water. And a glade opened up through the trees with a waterfall drowning out the sound of the drops falling as it was more a gasp of nature's power but tempered with the knowledge that it could not know everything.

"It's the Mithomere," gasped Rod. "It was so near."

"How did you know?" asked Endell, "You reckoned nothing save by sound."

"We have travelled but little distance," the wizard said. "And yet a distance of events from dread to dread. We can reckon our travel not through time but through the wild distortions of the magic woodland. It destroys our sense of space and proportion, though it matters not as we have found our goal. Do not forget your fear, this is the Mithomere. It is dangerous to those who guard not their thoughts or wonders."

And with his words the true splendor of the place flooded their view and understanding. Seeing it alone revealed truth they had not admitted even to themselves. Each thought they had was transformed into a gem of understanding with high value. Most of the group merely stood agape, unsure of what they were experiencing.

And there were so many insights, so much clarity into their past actions that they could not appreciate the depth of understanding they had entered into. They undervalued the knowledge they gained because it came so easily, without warning, nor explanation. For each truth shot out like a blaze of light into the full reality of their lives and the world, shedding even more understanding upon those things which concerned them.

The weak minded among them, the young squires particularly did not have the power to direct the oracle to the truth they sought. But the oracle did respond to their fear of it and respect for its thoughts.

There was a low waterfall that was a backdrop to the mere, some distance back of the pool and feeding it so gently there was no ripple nor current. The mere reflected back to a watcher's eyes the truth of the future of past of things they might desired to know. A tear or bead of sweat could cause the pool to move but not to ripple as the stained surface did react to the human addition to its composition, often with three times the insight and power of a view on its own. Herorot counseled strongly against touching the surface or throwing anything in.

They all moved towards the edge and the mere itself remained unchanged, calm, belying the menace of its reputation and Herorot's warnings. It had always been there, a natural formation, but in ancient times, so long ago that details did not exist, the mere had been fashioned for viewing and outfitted with an arched plinth cantilevered over the water with a golden railing so those brave enough could lean out over its surface and gaze deeply into its lustrous liquid depths.

"Touch not the mere, say all accounts and stories, for each drop can produce a magic much deeper than peace or war, or love or hate. Perhaps the greatest fear of anyone is indifference. The mere has shown some to have no impact at all on their times or acquaintances. Such a revelation has destroyed some men."

"And liberated others," said Endell.

And Herorot motioned them away from the edge of the mere, saying that they must approach it with the proper mindset and with particular thoughts in their approach if they were to get the insight they craved.

And the company realized that the mere might reveal things not in the scope of their present quest and those things might adversely affect their thinking and action on the mission they had before them. Not all were sure they wanted to gaze into its oracle depths, content as they were with the shower of understanding that merely being in proximity to the mere had already provided.

"A wrong step could leave us without hope. And hope is a tiny thing when compared to the enormity of all emotion but it is strong enough when mastered, to control those emotions and direct them. Even in the greatest despair, hope is always there right in the face of disaster. It can be betrayed and crushed but never abandoned where even the slightest thing exists for it to impress upon, for if there is life, hope is always there too.

Herorot resolved to go first. He begged the company to watch him as he had been to the mere before and understood it.

"Each one of you have the answer you would like to hear already prepared in your mind. But your question lays bare your hope but not necessarily the answer you want."

Herorot moved steadily to the mere's edge. He was small and penitent, almost forgotten in the swirl of events, as his questions did not impinge on the reason they were there.

He fixed his gaze into the watery surface where once there had been a hint of a ripple in the reflection, now there was nothing to mar its perfect polished glass façade. Knowing he was looking for a deeper answer he tried to fix his gaze below the surface, into the depths of the pool.

And he found it, something grabbed his thought, he held it in ecstasy, turning it over and over rather than letting it go, first with his mind, and then with his form, his body writhed to hold on. He was sweating in effort but his effort merely slowed the destination of his vision as only the briefest suggestion in his conscience took him to where he was afraid to go.

His joy at the mere turned to horror, as his wild eyes bespoke a voiceless fear, and the company watched as his initial delight died. Despite his dread at what he might see, he was unable to break away from the mere, his mind welded to that which he had sought.

He had sunk to his knees as he watched and now he rose violently and screamed a single word before falling in a crumpled heap, senseless now but the connection with the oracle was broken.

No one moved to him, unsure if his time at the mere was over. He lay amidst the flagstones and dirt in silence, staring into the sky, unmoving until a trickle of blood emerged from his ear and gathered enough volume to trace itself down the line of his jaw where it followed its contour onto his neck.

At the blood the company erupted with fear, not knowing the meaning of his scream.

"Guilty," he had yelled in finality, as its horror turned into a long low moan of despair, ending only as his own epitaph, his own death was complete.

All the company looked at each other. The mere was powerful they knew but now they saw it could kill with judgment, with truth, with the finality of reality by triggering a person's own emotions.

And each man thought, who might go next? Some had considered attempting the mere but now were unsure of its menace. And to a man they all knew that the only person who could chance the mere was Endell. He could feel their gaze upon him. He knew it too, and though sobered by Herorot's display he knew it was his fate to chance the mere, and that in truth if he was to achieve the success he craved, he must put his fate into the hands of chance.

All eyes coalesced onto his face, to see a flicker of his thought. He betrayed nothing, though he was sure they could all hear his hard beating heart. And before that rumination of his chest was caught he leapt forward to fill the silence.

"I beseech you all, those with faint fortune, do not stand in fear. You have no fight here, no reason to take on the oracle of future knowledge. It is your decision. But for the company, for our quest, I will approach the mere. I see you brave knights. I have seen a magician's folly of believing he could force his will and penitence on the mere and its judgment. And I see our courage torn down and raped, our humiliation and our once happy hearts turned to fear, and our gaze unable to meet our foe until after that foe is beaten."

Endell brandished his sword and smote the air.

"To arms! For all that is sacred and fair. Remember we are here because a pestilence attacked us. It came without warning nor faced any opposition, and it engulfed our homes and our farms. It threatens our friends, families and our lives and futures. I shall stay here and gaze into the oracle mere, for I will not let our quest fade or fail. And our determination shall not be swayed or turned into a debacle of misguided chance or never ending rotating goals."

And he started to the mere in the highly charged silence, his men watching him fearlessly take on the mere, despite the crumpled lifeless form of Herorot still at its side staring blankly at the sky.

"Stop," said a voice quietly and then said it again, "Stop."

Endell slowly turned to face the sound.

And one knight stood now, his true stature revealed. He advanced to Endell's side and knelt before him.

"Lord, I must do this deed and I shall swear, in the presence of the oracle, of Mithomere I have been cast to fill this role. I must protect my liege lord, such things are written in the sacred rights of knights, of errantry. Oh yes, my lord, there are times when the King must lead his men to battle, he must take the first step and be the first one into the fray. And that time will come. But this is not that time."

And Endell looked long into heaven, and then cast his gaze down and looked into the face of Kevin a true knight.

"You are brave and true my friend. I have seen it before. But this is my duty, I have brought you here, I am here on behalf of my people and their lands. Everyman who wishes, who has the desire and bravery can sample the oracle if they choose. No one must and can choose not to look. It is not for all. If you have no pressing question of fate why look? And even with such a question, perhaps you do not want the answer the oracle might provide."

Kevin would not be deterred and strode stiffly toward the

mere casting aside his armor, his sword and spear as he walked. He knew such petty arms would do him no good in a battle with the oracle and his own fate.

He had his convictions and his belief in their depth. He did not fear the oracle would change him, using a smidgen of doubt that all men have in their choices. For he had embraced his doubt, used it to bolster his beliefs by holding it and defeating it in turn.

He stopped at the railing in front of the mere, turning his eyes to heaven as he steeled his thoughts away from fear and tragic consequence. He counted aloud from seven to one and then with all eyes upon him he knelt and reached for the water until he brushed its surface. Kevin was brash and young, and had more than a dash of rebel behind his eyes.

Herorot had warned them not to touch the mere as that direct connection was too deep for people to endure, but Kevin knew his fate and with the touch felt a silence creep through his mind, like a thought in itself, a meandering thought of silence looking for something.

A garden fair he saw, and through the trees and grass now revealed was a voice. And that voice laid bare his future and choice. The folly of his betrothed was revealed. She wanted security from her fears but had put them both at risk by trying to stop him from going with Endell to take on the danger that beset their lives.

And he was foolish to let that request stand as their lives would be difficult enough, even well armed and intentioned and together.

And he heard the mere say as his finger rippled the pure surface, that he must convince her that his battle at Endell's side was a battle for her security. The chill in her heart was only an expression of her desire for safety without fear. Convince her and her heart will melt.

And Kevin's reverie was done. His hand came away ever so slightly from the surface of the mere. And the mere was glass again. And he smiled, quite content in his knowledge.

The others gathered round in the silence, and gasped as it appeared his was in some unnatural state of joy.

"The mere, 'tis wise and worthy of fear, but I am through and my own path is clear," he said. "I must leave Lord Endell, for a short time, but I will return to this quest. I have an errand and my path is to Doral Castle. There I will wed my princess Laurel the most fair, and I will return to you with a lock of her hair as proof of my faith in this quest, which to you is straight forward and enduring."

And Endell smiled at him, "Harm not a hair of Laurel's wreath, it might draw unwanted looks. I am full sure of your faith to me and this enterprise, and know you will prove true to your word. Be off to your fate and your due."

Now Endell's smile waned, his task upon him and he knelt at the rail to crystallize his thought as he had no idea of his future other than his determination not to back away from it. He was only concerned at what he should do next and not fearful at all about the knowledge he would gain.

His mind was not connected to the mere as he thought, all he wanted was the solution to the peril of cold and snow that befell his friends and their farms.

His hand shook slightly as he reached down to touch, as his charges watched with wide eyes, as his four-fingered hand stopped inches above the surface.

The apparently bottomless pool began to glow with a faint yellow light, at first just under his hand, gaining depth and brightness and spreading around.

Endell's eyes went wide, he had not expected this reaction by the mere. He remained motionless.

His hope for the future and his horror at what might be were mixing in his sight and he was powerless to stop it.

The mere's bright water bubbled and boiled, just in the area under his fingers. But Endell remained unmoved, his fingers reaching to the surface. And then a hand emerged from under the water and it grabbed Endell's wrist with an unexpected strength. And Endell did not know what this portended.

Rodney whooped and clasped his sword and leaned out over the railing to unleash a blow with a great yell.

In the few moments in which Endell had been connected to the heart of the Mithomere the rush of prophesy made everything clear to him. He was provided a clarity of understanding denied to most who tried the mere. He saw his problem. He saw his future spelt out, displayed to him.

He would command vast armies. He would wear a crown. As the battle flags fluttered in front of the army of men, powerful nobles beholden to him, had gathered at his request to quell a fate of unimaginable power, far more compelling than just the bringer of winter.

And yet, the mere showed these truths but something more too. Endell saw that he faced a situation that was more than grim, where the nobles were there only in body not spirit and his battle hopes were balanced on a knife edge, despite appearances of the strength he brought to bear.

The army was roused before the dawn to prepare. And Endell was commanding but the mere showed that he was merely playing a part, and was a pawn in the greater game, the nature of which he could not penetrate nor understand.

He saw a messenger enter bringing news that Endell's allies had arrived and wanted to know the battle plan. And Endell in his vision allowed a calming smile to break his visage, a view of his kingly face as he said, "The tide has swung and we must take the fleeting opportunity to capitalize before our window is closed."

He told the messenger to return to the newly arrived and instruct them to encircle their foes and cut off their retreat. Without them he had no means of stopping his beaten foes from moving back and reforming for a second battle charge. And with them holding his foe in place he would lead a charge into the heart of their forces.

All this passed to Endell from the oracle in the time it took Rodney to react with his sword. Endell did not move as Rodney slashed at the hand that held Endell tight. At his stroke, aimed just below the surface of the mere, the connection with the mere was broken. And with the break in his vision the battle's result was not revealed.

But with that stroke through the water, the splash drew him into the oracle's power, his skin speckled with droplets holding him in its grip.

Rodney's eyes rolled back into his head, and he sank to the ground, to all eyes he was dead, crumpled like Herorot nearby. Endell had barely moved, only drawing back his hand from the carnage, and holding it up to see a long cut, which displayed his blood. The hand which he had held was no longer to be seen.

But no blood dripped from so violent a wound. And no sooner did his companions see the cut, as they gasped in shock as the cut knit itself together and disappeared before them as if it had only happened in a dream.

And with that Endell returned to the present and turned to Rodney whose crumpled body lay near. His eyes were wide open but unseeing as if he had been struck a blow so terrible that it's concussive force had killed him.

Endell bent to close his former squire's eyes and tried again until he realized that Rodney was yet alive though he was convulsed into a statue. The Mithomere held him in its grasp. Endell ordered a member of the company to take Rodney away from the side of the mere. He knew that Rodney would be revived as he thought back to the what the mere had shown him, the battle preparations with Rodney by his side.

And so Endell conceived to return to his castle. The mere indicating that the snow and cold were natural and posed no long term threat, and that he must prepare for the real danger to come.

The visions in the mere had given Endell the courage of foreknowledge, as he thought his fate would be well despite his blindness as to the outcome of the great battle.

He still had to make it all happen. He did not know how he would lead, how it would happen that he would be king. And the battle plan displayed and allies drawn did not provide the complete picture he craved. He knew he must prepare diligently, assuming nothing. And still he thought that with such preparation he could not fail, the oracle had indicated.

The Mithomere had played its trick and altered Endell's perception of the future. Reality to come now existed in Endell's mind and heart as he believed with conviction all the steps of what had been, what was staring him in the face and what the Mithomere had suggested, would come to pass.

The speckled drops on Rodney dried and as they did the squire came back to waking.

"I have seen our lands free of snow, the menace of the cold removed by Endell's actions."

And the rest of the company cheered both Rod's return to the living and his assertion that all was well and their quest complete. They were eager to be finished with the snow, the cold, and the oddities of magic and prophesy.

And as the company gathered to move away from the Mere, Rodney spoke quietly to Endell.

"And there is more, too horrible to speak of. For if my vision is true then our future is bleak."

And Endell was happy as he believed his future secure.

"What did you see? Was it your death perhaps or was it me?"

Rodney for his part stayed silent. Endell took the signal.

"But Rod, I will die, someday. Were there indications of when or where or how or why?"

"You are right of course, there was not time indicated nor reason. In my sight you wore a crown with an inlay of Avowan, and you were older and careworn but still armed with a blade. Your death must be heroic or at time's end as our symbol Avowan allows no despair."

Endell was secretly pleased with this foretelling, as it seemed to him that his power and prestige were growing and that it portended a height of renown beyond his hopes, that he Endell would wear a crown and lead all men.

"Well the snow is cast down. Be it by the Mere by our willingness to challenge the problem and face evil as it hunted us down, or perhaps it was Herorot, unknowingly the clown of such choice. But we appear to have triumphed, so let us take thanks in our success and move back to our homes to enjoy it. Even young Kevin can rejoice as he can leave us on his errand without feeling that he abandoned our goal."

The ragged party moved through the wood, spent from their adventures. They didn't worry about their path, only concerned that their direction was true and that they put distance behind them. They spoke about their future and their present around the fire that night, with all hoping they would soon find themselves in familiar lands.

It was difficult for the party to find their way as the woodland was dense and the canopy full, so finding the direction of the sun was difficult as they could not track its movements.

And Endell was not concerned as he had seen the future and felt it was going to be good for him. He praised the group for their success in ending the cold, even though many of the company had not seen any direct evidence that they had actually achieved anything.

The next morning the band tried to get a sun bearing and used the gentle breeze to suggest a course. It's warm lilt gave credence to Endell's supposition that the evil cold had been mastered.

Endell took the opportunity of a rest in their journey to climb a nearby crest to look as far as he could above the tree line. And he gazed to the east and saw autumn fields full of harvest, a sight which shocked him.

"Autumn, how can that be. We left in winter and have spent little more than a fortnight, perhaps two if our reckoning was wrong. And it appears that more than half a year has passed."

"It seems that time has gotten away from us," said Rod. "Our marches have taken much time, how I do not know, as we only stopped for nightfall a score of times at most."

There was a curious look to the fields and Endell returned to the camp with a shout, they were about to enter their own lands, and their fields and farms were free of snow and laden with ripe corn, and other things that had grown in their absence.

As they moved forward the company rejoiced to see Endell was right. And as they marched on their way to see the King, local farmers, and villagers came to see them and cheered their approach, giving them food and garlands and leading them in songs of victory and deliverance.

And the people fell in behind the travelers in revelry.

"O'er lands known to deeds renown, Forward, Forward, We never look down," the company sang. "Through tended field under clear bright skies, Forward, Forward until we die."

They declaimed their victory and their right to enjoy its fruits. They insisted they would do it all again but now they were wiser in the ways of battle.

As they traveled, more and more people joined their group, some left as they were far from home, but their numbers swelled. News of their coming ran far ahead of them, causing some of the churches to ring their steeple bells in celebration, as many had seen the change in their fortunes but wondered for many weeks what had happened to Endell's party.

They stopped often as villagers beckoned them to rest and take food and drink. Endell wanted to allow his men to have their moment of victory even though he knew it delayed their arrival at the King's castle.

The toast was consistent to one and all, "To the heroes of

Gremquest, each and all." Endell took great joy in the celebrations and pleasure of the small folk.

As they approached Endell's Castle Gremquest a horseman thundered on approach, riding hard. He reined his mount through the dust he raised, dismounted and bowed low.

"I am a messenger Royal. Loyal to the crown and sent to deliver these words . . . 'Hail Endell, our thanks and faith rewarded. At your leisure come to me and allow me to fete you and your company for your service. On top of my hospitality, titles shall be bestowed and rewards given. To Endell the title Duke of Gremquest shall be. Others will be awarded once we have heard and digested your adventurous tales."

And the Royal countenance fell, as the official duties had been performed. And the messenger broke into a wide smile, matched by Endell, as the company all rose in one voice of joy.

"Thank you my good knight," shouted Endell above the din. "Tell the King of my most humble fear and acceptance of his judgment on this bequest. At his request we will proceed to him quickly after visiting our own homesteads and kin and making ourselves presentable to him."

The knight thundered away and the company cheered again at Endell's quiet judgment, allowing them time at home.

"To Gremquest with haste," directed Endell. "Our winter discontent is past and so is the magic that fueled it."

And his horse leapt away with Rodney in pursuit and in the dust they raised followed the rest of the company and happy locals.

Their whooping display was borne of the breeze to Gremquest itself, audible to the guards on the walls, though far away still.

A sentry noticed it first and then recognized it for the joy it expressed. and before long the dust in the distance spoke of the return of Endell.

The sentry wasted no time in rousing the Castle.

"Awake awake, to our great joy, Lord Endell returns."

He called for a triumphant reception to meet the master of the Castle, noting they had barely an hour to prepare, given the size of the dust mote on the horizon.

Roused to action the Castle and its inhabitants moved with speed, knowing that Endell would want a celebration and knowing the speed of Garland his mount.

They were right, Garland covered the ground before an hour had passed. And the Castle lay in silence. Not even sentries appeared.

Endell furrowed his brow and stood with Garland at the foot of the drawbridge assessing what he saw, strong walls, and no sign of human habitation. Was his victory mooted by some disaster at home? As he wondered Rodney caught him, and the rest of his company arrived in twos and threes.

"There is no one to meet us at our journey's end?"

Rodney cantered about, unsure of what to do.

And then a trumpet blasted from the battlement wall, and the Avowan banner was run up the pole atop the highest tower.

Endell grinned as the drawbridge dropped and people appeared, pouring forth from the castle and making themselves visible on the battlements and in high windows. At a call they all loudly cheered as one voice.

And in the congratulations and joy Endell looked for Evelyn but could not see her. In a fit of determination he declared he would not enter the Castle until he had met with the King and knew his will. He pitched a camp near the drawbridge and said he would stay until such business as was necessary was complete.

The people made merry into the next day but Evelyn remained apart and Endell was concerned and upset, thinking perhaps something terrible had happened while he was away, and the people feared to tell him.

He finally asked a young lad, "Where is she, has something bad happened?"

The young boy told him what he had heard from his own mother, that Evelyn remained in her rooms and it is told that she pines for the companies return, but will not come to meet it, instead wanting you to approach her, as waiting for so long was difficult for all.

"Her maids do tell that she refuses to move first upon your return. She is claiming a sickness from the prick of a sword she had moved to display."

But Endell knew the truth because he knew Evelyn well. He rolled his eyes at her display but told the boy not to mention that he snuck into the Castle to assuage her and console.

"It is for her only that I break my word on entering the pile of stone."

He pulled a hood up over his face, and the cloak seemed to fade to a deeper shadowy gray. He slipped into the Castle, showed himself to the guards at her rooms, and they nodded that they would keep his secret, happy that he saw fit to make this visit and not dig in too deeply on his plans.

He crept into the room but she was asleep. He reached his hand to rouse her, wanting to get to the end of her consternation, but he stopped his hand.

He looked at her, asleep, all fear fallen from her face. And he thought how easily he had won her love and how much he now valued it, despite its natural ease. And he kissed her brow and sang softly a lay.

"Awake when your love returns your kiss. He is here and nothing is amiss. Awake with a smile to match my own, and rejoice with me, your love is come home."

Her eyes fluttered but remained closed. He wondered a moment but saw her fight to keep her eyelids down and he smiled seeing through her ploy, singing the verse again, only a touch louder.

She smiled widely the game complete.

"Awake my love I am back from my test and we must travel to see the King."

She still did not move and Endell implored her, first patiently and then by seizing her waist and tickling her until she begged him to stop, with a laugh on her lips.

"Meet me astride your mount tomorrow and we will ride to the King, happy to have completed our quest and deliver the people and their farms from the strange cold. It is said that we will be anointed Duke and Duchess by our generous King, though I fully expected his appreciation."

Evelyn was bewitched enough that she dismissed her concern at Endell's sense of entitlement for his actions, actions that appeared to have fallen in his lap rather than been fought for.

And so, as the next day dawned, Evelyn was fitted out for a ride. She cantered down the drawbridge of Gremquest, toward the encampment of Endell and his company. She moved silently without banners or trumpets announcing her arrival, only the soft clip clop of her horse's hooves, which echoed on the stone roadway and wooden beams of the bridge.

And as she stayed her mount a fanfare did echo from the battlements, and Endell appeared and for a long second he stared at her, remembering her beauty as the rising sun lit her up. But he remembered his duty and began to complete it.

"Beautiful you are," he could think of nothing else to say. "How could I have left you while I completed my task?"

He shook his head remembering the danger they believed lurked behind the magic severity of cold and snow. But he silently pledged to never leave her behind again, and his ambition would be muted and perhaps even shelved.

He decided that she was his pledge, her safety his employ. And while he felt she was safe at Gremquest, even that strong castle was not impervious to battle. She was his first charge no matter what else may come. And fate, as displayed by the Mere, would align his future and provide the necessary conditions for him to achieve his destiny.

And Endell took to Garland and they slowly moved as one over the pleasant green lands of autumn. The only thing in their way was the thanks of small folk and town's people who came out to bow their heads in thanks. But soon they managed to reach the King's lair, his golden hall where he sat upon a gilded chair to receive visitors and petitions from near and far. His crown, a heavy golden, jewel encrusted affair, was displayed upon a felt orb up and behind his place. He wore it when necessary but preferred to show it as a talisman of his station and power.

"All Hail the King," shouted a helmeted guard and all in the space rose as one as the King entered from a small alcove near the chair.

A bard stationed in front of the dais began a lay of welcome, "All praise our most reverend monarch and listen at his command to the Lay of Endell. And the singer told of battles and fury causing no end of concern to Endell who knew such trifles to be inventions as the song troubled over his battle decisions and field actions.

At its end the King spoke, "Hail Endell, Lord Protector of the Realm. In the wake of your overwhelming deeds and service to us, I name you my heir. What title would you like? A Duke you can be. An Earl. Or more if you desire. While you think on it, all hail Endell the next king!"

The surprise of the announcement shook everyone there. The king took his sword and laid it on both of Endell's broad shoulders silently saying the words of commitment to his choice. "It is done."

And the hall rose in tumult of joy but Endell stood in the center of the storm shocked at this choice of the King. So he would be the next king, but was that where his path and legend was supposed to lead?

"All hail the next King. You managed overwhelming deeds. We do not know where you came from but you have established our trust with your deeds on our behalf. Return to Gremquest but visit us often. I've much to teach you ere the end of my days."

And the feasting and games went on for days barely counted until Endell and Evelyn made their way back to Gremquest. The news of the investiture traveled before them and they were hailed double now.

And as they approached their castle a mob approached to meet them with joy and happiness overflowing as all of them knew that good would come of their association with the next king. Word had traveled to them with speed and they knew more than even Endell who had not being gathering information from many sources as had they.

In this happiness Evelyn swooned, and taking a bit of drink was able to say, "Oh the joy of it, how happy I am."

And the crowds swelled the castle which was decorated with many things but most prominently an array of Avowan in full bloom. Balloons, food and drink, displays of arms, music; nothing was forgotten, right down to games of chance, amusements for children and food for their beasts.

Endell had chosen the titles Duke of Gremquest and Earl of Avowan among lesser notations of his deeds, such as the Marquis of Mithomere and Marshall of the Forest.

Endell was dressed in finery at Evelyn's request, but he chafed at the cloth, though he tried to enjoy its fit and feel. He shared widely with all in attendance but his own purse was not enough to keep up such appearances, and he preferred to be at one with his people. Though Endell began to enjoy the fineness and slowly understood that the common people liked a King in finery, such a thing was a reflection of their own desires and perceptions.

And so he began to live like a King and thought of living higher still, but wondered what he could achieve to bring on more adulation.

He wracked his brains and his past and wondered what he could do that would bring him more fame and immortality.

And while he thought, he strengthened his place, visiting the King, progressing around the realm, and increasing his stature by recasting his lance Endurendil. He fashioned it into a thing of gold, a romance of jewels. Once a solid piece of strongest wood, it was now adorned with so much show that it seemed absurd, no longer a fighting weapon but a trophy on his shelf.

And he knew that true fighting men fight not with ornaments or works of art that can be bought from a smith. He knew that fighting men take their hearts and what weapons they can muster and handle at need.

And thinking such things he dreamed as he gazed from the battlements each day, that someday he would ride Garland to battle once more, fair deeds to accrue.

Through autumn he dreamed every night of battles with monsters, with evil and with the elements. And in his dreams, from the west arose a great haze, with thunder, earth shaking rattles and booms that continued for days on end.

It was an army, so vast that no one in it knew of its beginning or end. They did not know who led it but they did know their destination. And Endell smiled at the dream thinking that his visage commanded the horde to home. They were returning home to Gremquest. But then his vision did falter, they returned in defeat, untold thousands were dispersed and in flight from their foes and could only bleat out their desire for home and peace.

Endell awoke from this nightmare bathed in a stinging sweet sweat. He knew it was no dream but a prescient vision of the future.

His plans for glory lay precarious, broken on his view of the future. And he knew that if the plans did fade and die, his life, his achievements, titles and history would disperse on the breeze. He knew his own history and knew that courage was called upon, even if the changes he had wrought were remembered, it all hung on the outcome of his dream. He could not relive his glorious deeds he had to create new ones, and at that his courage grew holes, as he feared losing all he had won.

And before this host could find Gremquest a messenger from the King arrived. The King was dead. The Endell of so long ago was crowned and was King and was given the name - King Arrol - exactly as Evelyn had prophesied so long ago.

And the years since this deed he remembered. The years of joy of desire for more but nothing to show save a parade of feasting and of avarice, and merciful judgments.

And so Arrol King, once Endell the strong, girt on his armor, light yet strong, and experienced by him only in song and tournament. At first he feared he had become soft, but as he completed the task his courage rose, he sang battle songs finishing as he took his crown and fixed his sash of rank.

A trumpet call blared from nearby calling the men to arms, to mount their steeds and ready for battle.

Arrol bent his head, vowing to make peace by dispatching his enemies and then among his people. And as he prepared a young knight approached him. Kevin was there to help, despite his love for his lady he loved battle too, though he bore no favor of his lady, she understood his need to go but would not sanction it with any symbol.

"Hail, King Arrol, rest easy, your fame is assured. We will fight for our own stories and for more chances for honor and glory. I am honored to fight with you, this the 13th time I have saddled up in your service."

And Kevin gave him an idea. There was a dell formed some distance away, and by positioning themselves inside the dell, the huge army might be able to come at them from all sides but would be limited to the size of the dell, in effect, evening the numbers of those who could lend their arms at any one time.

Their enemies would have no choice but to assail them in this fashion, and with their success growing the dead piled at their feet would make attack even more difficult.

"The huge army, it is moving," Kevin said at the sound of hooves and clashing steel.

"I lead," screamed Arrol, spurring ahead, "I lead and always have and will until I cannot lead anymore."

And he spurred Garland away, pushing past his men and moving into the dell where the battle was already joined. He charged down the slope, slicing past soldiers thick as snowflakes. He slashed, thrust in battles without breaking, toward the flag of his enemy king, already at the bottom of the dell. King Arrol was spurred on by his knowledge that within this battle was his destiny, and by his boast of superiority. He moved easily to the banner, untouched and unbowed, like a ghost through the battle as it raged, almost magical in its effortless flow.

He arrived at the center, the bottom of the dell. The battle all around him seemed to fade away. He was left with only a single warrior to combat. And this mounted king appeared almost mystical, purer than the light.

Nothing was said, and no movements were made and yet Arrol knew that this was a battle for his destiny, his due of glory stood at the end of this encounter.

Arrol looked closely at his foe. He was familiar in a way Arrol could not express. He had no talisman, no sign or sigil from which to identify him. In truth, Arrol knew not who this army was, why they had come to challenge him nor why they were about to fight. He even thought for a moment to offer an alliance but dismissed the thought as absurd as the battle raged around them.

After silently eyeing him, the other king deliberately drew his sword. Arrol was unmoved. He remained frozen in his destiny.

And the other king's blade glinted in the sun blinding Arrol. And with the flash of light in his eyes the truth of his life flashed before him and his destiny too and his memories faded as he lived them, like a handful of dust sparkling in a beam of light and falling to earth gently, floating through the beam and out of the light.

End Part Two

Canto III

King Arrol came back to consciousness in a swath of grass, looking up at the firmament.

He remembered there had been a battle but could not perceive of his actions in it. Did he win or lose, were his men victors? His mind was blank to anything but the sky, the grass sward he lay upon and the sound of running water.

He glanced around and could see evidence of the battle and he thought he heard distant clashes of steel and grunts of men.

And then he knew he was stripped of his armor, only clad in his mortal honor and the virtue that he had built during his lifetime of deeds.

He had been given the chance that all men had when they wake to the world. The battle remained in front of him but his banner was still wrapped tightly. There were no trumpets to announce the contestants and no one around to watch the proceedings save memories and ghosts.

And yet he laid still, without perceptible sound but the air was clean and heavy with some will, some purpose that was far stronger than the presence of anyone person or even a whole army of noble personages with long pedigrees of action and achievement.

And the firmament above gave no depth, no band of cloud, no star did peek. It was a uniformly bland lighted space, giving everything enough light to see but not dazzle. The horizon was near because he lay at the bottom of a bowl-shaped dell, familiar it was. But beyond the rim of the dell, far in the distance were mountains and between the hint of streams and rivers and forests, scattered on the wind.

"The battle must have swept by since I fell, but what of this place, I remember it not. Was I carried from the battle and left to rot in this unwholesome place? Or has some other fate befallen me? I beg God for answers, details from which to parse out the truth."

As he took it in, the landscape remained unchanged, though to his sight and fading memory it was just different enough that he felt as if he was in another world.

He thought back to the battle and the splendor of his knights, battle pennants floating on their staves, and the raging clash of arms, but he could not perceive an outcome. He saw only that it came to a final fight between him and the unknown king. But of that fight he remembered nothing and the whole affair was fading from his memory even as he tried to recall it.

"I could easily forget the hell of it and would invite my brain to let that go, forever gone so no moment could bring it back to me."

And he knew that broken bodies are the payment of crusades on battlefields in protest lines. That death was the payment of war, and before the victor is determined battle and war are about screaming pain, and the moans of final breaths. He had to wonder how he had avoided that. That no bodies lay around. That he was all alone and obviously allowed to be so by something more powerful than he.

Arrol thought to rise and start a search to understand his fate. He looked around the entire circle once completely, taking note of any detail. He thought of his home at Castle Gremquest and the surrounding Garadreium Wood and other tangible things that were familiar to him. And having risen, each step he took restored some memory but he was unable to put those memories into an coherent narrative of his life.

His memories were so whole and complete; each kiss, each decoration or scream of pain was so clear that he was forced to try to place them and to understand the workings of his active mind.

With each step something new was cast and with these things came emotions in sharp detail.

He lived each moment of the battle in a picture perfect memory of detail, like his mind was being trawled for details he had seen or touched or smelled, but had not otherwise penetrated his conscience. He began to see very clearly in his mind's eye.

And as he walked he emerged from the dell and approached a pool of the bluest water, and there, seemingly waiting for him, was a local king's nymph daughter. He did not know how he knew of those details. She was young, naïve but learned, and Arrol was still in a sort of trance, unsure what was real or a dream.

He lifted his eyes from the ground he had been walking and locked on to her royal blue orbs. Much as he knew exactly who she was, he knew that she would be there and that she was waiting for him.

"All the thoughts and memories and perceptions of my life are complete but what has it gained me?" he asked.

"Do you consider the view of your life bothersome? In all our lives there are times which are better seen from a distance, with proper perspective. Other things we lived, some joys and wonderment, lay forgotten and dusty, dry mutations of our eventual understanding, shards left behind as we learn. And though we thirst for this knowledge we dismiss the path that found it for us, the path that revealed it. Why do we dismiss the wonder and joy of discovery?"

She pointed out that people can easily remember those times when their plans or hopes did not work out, where effort was wasted. It is our tale of woe, she explained, and a true grief but it is not what terrifies us.

"It is the fear of death that transfixes us, as self preservation is our highest command, and is given to all beasts in proportion to their awareness. Sometimes it defines them. In lower orders of beasts it is there but only as a sliver of their conscious being as if unbeing is just as natural. Do you fear death King Arrol?"

"I am a man and my life is my work, day after day."

"But do you fear your own death? Do you fear the end, the horrible idea that life will not go on?"

And Arrol explained that without his life he would not be able to defend his life and deeds, his reason for living, so he did not fear its end.

"Once my spirit leaves me then I cannot be anymore, though my ghost may remain to pay some price. And though you speak of it so strangely, I do not expect death shall catch me yet as I am in the prime of my life."

With that he smiled wide, a capture of his courage. But she looked at him with such a questioning gaze that his smile faded and he knew he needed answers to this fate.

"I have never seen nor heard of this place nor any like it. Where are we? What is this place?"

"In this place you have been many times, both alone and with Garland your bold mount. Yet you can only perceive of now because other times were in dreams or hidden in vows. It is higher than your mind or heart and still more common than birth."

"Was I evil, despite my many glorious righteous deeds, both quietly done or widely known?"

Arrol explained he tried to do justice in small things and in larger deeds and accomplishments, and he rode with his trusted steed Garland, and virtue which bestowed favor of fate upon him and his deeds. He explained he trusted councils even if he held violent answers to his will in his sword hand. He admitted to a few indiscretions but in his heart he knew they were mistakes and had sought forgiveness from himself, as he understood the problem and vowed to never again made those errors.

"Merely admitting your foul deeds does not exorcise them," the nymph girl said. "We must make restitution and fully correct our wrongs and not select our own penance at a convenient moment. Lavishing love or spending excessively does not cleanse the error. The mistake must be righted and more besides."

She explained to him that he was not banished to Hell as his conscience in these matters had saved him from that fate.

And Arrol was pleased, thinking himself bounded to eternal paradise. He explained that he was tormented by his mistakes and sins large and small but had no idea that this torment would save him from eternal damnation.

"Have you failed to listen? You have made a particular lifelong vow and your true test remains ahead and very soon, as you have missed damnation by a sliver. And pass this test and you may receive eternal bliss."

She said that paradise for Arrol was still within his grasp but the race he would run would be difficult as his desires would be muted by his abilities. If he could win in whatever form a win might take by displaying a true heart, he would be granted his wish to be exalted as a champion on Earth and his star would grow brighter, and in paradise he would be contented by his life well spent.

And she explained that this test was conducted on a fighting field but he would be without armor or sword or shield.

"So it is a war of words or some mental fight that I must pass in order to achieve my self-imposed destiny. For it is now obvious that I am dead to my old life and will never again push a pen or pull a plough. Strange it is that I would say that, as I never did those things, though they seem like joys now that they are beyond me. I always thought of life like a perfect flower, cultivated, beautiful, held high, and defended. Most lovely when considered with an uncluttered mind."

She told him that it was not a mental fight he would engage in.

"You will fight a physical test and if you refuse, look about you, you are bound here until the battle is complete and you have victory or defeat, and your destiny complete."

She offered him the opportunity to ask questions and to follow her if he wanted. She walked through a land without discernible feature. Without streams, nor mountain, nor trees. Nothing but broken land. It was not a place that life could be sustained. The land was as dead as anyone who passed through it. And after a time of walking they chanced upon a steep mound which had columns at the top supporting a stone roof. This shrine marked and guarded a door which the nymph said was the entrance to her father's palace.

She swept her hand toward the door and bade Arrol to enter. She told him to beware of anything he encountered save her father the King, as only he had the power to remove the taint of evil. And she wished him luck on his quest and moved back down the slope.

"What is this place?" Arrol gestured at the door and then all around him.

"It is the place of the stepping stone." She was solemn and spoke quietly. After speaking she turned back to move away and quickly melted out of sight into the mindscape and low light.

Arrol knew he was on the threshold of eternity and could naught but face it. As he reached for the door it swung wide open. A long hall stretched far into the hill but it wasn't empty. Adorning the way there was a carnival of characters of all shapes, sizes and demeanors that came and went up and down the hall, into doors and out. A constantly changing crowd, everyone with a place to go or be.

Despite the menagerie, Arrol moved as if blind through the door, feeling little trust in what he saw and touching all about to see if it was real. Each movement, each step was an adventure and he felt like a thief in the midst of his crime.

A man appeared and asked him what he sought.

"I have a place to hide besides my own," he said. " 'Tis safe and strong as stone."

"I am not hiding and I do not fear, save the lack of light. I advance to the King for a talk, I am not trying to leave."

"Oh you are a brave soul. I have talked with the King too and after that conversation I decided to stay here rather than chance eternal darkness by remaining in limbo in this crazy place."

The man explained that the option to fight for one's destiny is always available but remaining in that place seemed better than facing evil and darkness and battle.

"I am rational and at peace with my choice, though I admit I turn over the decision in my mind constantly. You need to think about your desires before agreeing to face the fight for your life."

And as others drew close to them he smiled a wide grin ignoring them all.

Arrol enquired how to find the King as he wanted to hear the facts from him before the recommendations of those who chose to remain in that place had festered into something other than advice.

"You are under the spell of the blue eyed nymph girl. But what powers can she have as she is only a spirit and not a living human being as were we all?"

He explained that only personal will had any currency in that place as not even love itself could intrude, as all the spirits feared it. The test would be on his mind and heart by pressuring with fear to push those tested away from the peace of death to its tragedy.

"You have said you would go on, it is your own words I heard, and I will lament you but will not cry, because if all had courage like you, what would courage be? Certainly not a virtue if everyone possessed it, it would be part of us, part of our being, like a finger or hair on our heads." And he started away, down the hallway.

Arrol followed on thinking this person was leading him, but he turned off the straight path just as the hall took on a character of a passage in a great castle. He waved Arrol on having made his choice. Arrol passed groups of people who didn't take notice of him, not realizing that he was different from them. they could not discern between those who had a choice to make and those who had made it.

And as he walked he wondered if he really was unlike all the loiterers he passed, who had no clear goal. As he approached the throne and the King upon it, the loiterers were fewer, though they took notice of the audience about to begin. They remained in the shadows, vicariously existing on the edge of someone else's choices, rather than deign to face their own destiny and pay the price of paradise.

Arrol moved through the halls and his blood became icy with his determination. That change in countenance became apparent as with each room he passed more and more people took notice of him. They could feel his determination. He was looking for his destiny but still was not bound to chase it. He looked for a sign to direct his choice as the value of it bounced back and forth in his mind, neither choice winning out.

He was summoned by a voice from the next room, the final room at the end of the hallway. He knew this was his moment. He felt the weight of doom despite his corporeal bravery and the fact that his terrestrial accomplishments were now firm in his mind.

The room he entered was bare, save for a fantastical throne and the King who sat upon it, unmoving. Fighters and warriors came to this place but the King on the throne had never seen battle, only its result. He did not encourage fights knowing that they resulted in broken men, in mind, spirit and body, and supplied him with more supplicants than he wanted.

Though Arrol did not comprehend, all the citizens of this realm lacked faith in themselves and their choices and so had become wraiths who fear to fight but remained to complain and sneer at those who would face their own destinies. These wraiths would seethe at their own failures, as each victory they may have had and the loss of their own souls, which by their actions they swept to blackness.

They believed their own kingly leader had not spelt out the

consequence of their death in battle. They fell down the well of eternity even if they fought well, their service exemplary, they still had to take the choice of battling for their eternal soul. And so they stayed in limbo, fearing beyond death to make a choice of folly and see it face to face.

And the King of this underworld waved Arrol forward, claiming they had business to discuss.

"I can answer your questions but I will never force you to make a choice."

And Arrol wanted this man, this King to identify himself, to come clean on who and what he was, as Arrol said he came to this parlay without pretense, his cards on the table and his conscience clear on the aspects of his life that now seemed in question.

"I'm afraid that you comprehend little," said the King, who identified himself as Pellas, Lord of the Middle Kingdom.

He told Arrol he could call him anything as long as it befit his station and was not insulting. He explained that in that place he was the authority but really he was just a caretaker of it to those who passed through, which is what Arrol was at that moment, even if he had a greater claim than most, to whatever lay beyond.

He gestured Arrol to sit and they spoke in jests and dueled in generous and happy accord displaying their wits and knowledge.

After a time Arrol said, "My liege lord, why is it that such a fine man as you is the lord of all this woe and discord?"

And a shade passed the light of the space and the room hushed in surprise, yet the effect did not last.

"Say not that name in these halls , for Woe is at the bottom of the cataract, the river fall. But lay your questions aside a moment as I relay a tale.

"Once on a small northern farm a boy purchased a drink from a peddler which was tainted with death. Both his parents took mighty draughts and died. The boy did not expect poison had come in the drink. He went to live with his grandmother and worked her farm alone and despite his youth and strength he was haunted by the sudden loss of his parents.

And people around knew his story and tried to do things for him to ease his pain, but their efforts were in vain. And he was outwardly appreciative of their efforts but he feigned his thanks as he was fearful that any lasting connection would be destroyed by fate and his heart would be broken again.

"And that boy forged an empire from the farm, doing it without crossing anyone or doing them any injustice. And yet the tragedy lay heavy upon him, so much so, that he refused to marry. Though he was rich in goods he was not particularly wise in all things. He had forgotten love and forsaken the central role it plays in our actions and hopes.

"He did not indulge in anything that might soften his heart, or allow a crack of compassion to enter him, all for fear of bereavement.

"And I know this tale well, down through the emotions of the poor boy who became so hardened by fear. I know because I was that boy. And I have, since my life, been sent here to preside over this play which allows no joy. There was no sin nor indiscretion that I committed, and yet I was full of folly, which I understand now. Perhaps I will be able to move on sometime but not until my former spirit is dead and completely removed from my soul. I have long been King here and likely will be for much longer as I am a monument to the pull of the heart losing to the distilled logic of the brain."

"But what of the nymph, your daughter, how is that so?"

"She is but another with woe, and seeks to hide behind my shield," and he laughed aloud. "She did incline to hide her love so fearful was she of rejection. A quest for popularity replaced the need for a human connection. She sought the admiration of the crowd rather than the mightier emotion of a single soul. Many out there count themselves as my progeny, the ones who reject the notion of the need for emotion."

And Arrol asked after the need for the physical test and wanted to know about all the potential details of such a contest.

King Pellas wanted to know if Arrol understood why he was in such a place.

And Arrol told him that he could rest before his final test and gain immortality if he was successful or fade to blackness if he was not. And the third way was simply not to choose and remain a shade without admiration or tears of anyone he encountered.

"You can choose your time to fight but I warn you, there will be a winner and a loser. Your opponent is set as an equal peer, especially chosen for you, not a simple farmer nor merchant, you will battle a fighting man of stature which will harness your fear and force you to keep your wits if you are to win the day.

"And if you fail, you will be forced to the edge of the precipice and you will be swept away by the river and carried to the cataract which will spill you to eternal strife, to the real Lord of Woe who awaits the fallen at the canyon's bottom. You will be treated with hatred as the most recent inhabitant to experience the world without complete fear, hatred and evil and you will slowly inexorably lose your connection to it and become one of them."

Arrol knew now that the seemingly weak choices of those who remained in this plain were those of people who felt they could not win a place in paradise, who feared failure and evil more than they thirsted for honor and joy.

"The battle is found on a small island, Aaon, which rises in the middle of the river like a crest, long but narrow, flat but never subsumed in the stream. There is a strong current on both sides of the island. The fight is more than just a test of physical strength. It will bare the soul and show the true nature of will of those engaged."

Pellas told that no weapons were allowed each participant except their own bodies and minds and the experiences of their lifetimes. You will be shod and dressed very simply and masked so you cannot know your opponent, nor he you, nor see his grimace or laughter.

It is possible that you met this warrior in life and so knowing him might tip the scales of advantage.

And Arrol boldly proclaimed that he would enter the fight as soon as it could be prepared. And to Pellas he wondered aloud why his throne room was so bare and why there was no sustenance available other than the honest talk.

"My whole life has led me here. I have been compelled by some unseen force to do those things I have done which resulted in this moment."

Arrol said he was resolved to make the attempt and wanted to make it soon, as every moment he spent in the Middle Kingdom made it easier to forgo his destiny and remain a wraith in that place.

"It is my only hope. My only way to avoid the end of my rope, or by taking on the resolution find it one way or another." Arrol looked around and saw that everyone in the room except Pellas had averted their gaze, and could not look him in the eye.

And Pellas sighed and agreed with Arrol that the only way to break the spirit of its torpor was to challenge your destiny and agree to the battle. He acknowledged that as a King in life he had a true resolve but wondered if the feelings in his heart matched those of his soul.

"In this fight you cannot trust old passions to react the same as they have ever. In the heat of the moment your heart and soul may not be in line together. Your stand here has revealed a new and intense emotion which is different than you have had before, before you had to consider the ultimate meanings of your actions. But I grant your request, a fight you shall have."

Pellas beckoned Arrol to come and be prepared and advised caution or the fight for his soul would be short.

And Arrol was arrayed with a white cloth and shirt and shod for quick movement with a heavy flap of armor. He wore a light red sash from his left shoulder to his chest which provided a small pocket. It was the only identifying mark upon him. He was given a short time to consider his strategy but he could not really know it until he was in the arena. Try as he did his thought kept returning to the bare bones of his life.

"Oh death, that void upon the open ocean, where souls slowly make for some distant land or idea of it. How can I hold those conscious memories, my motivations and mistakes? He was attached to his past life and the possibility that he would disappear and miss paradise and be removed even from the devil's grasp into nothingness. And he thought that constant bliss would reduce the worth of bliss and may even make heaven a hell, and hell itself a welcome respite, where at least he had something tangible.

"It is change that drives the engine of our lives. It is the variation from horror to joy, and the vibrant strings of that change in both directions which make life the splendor that it is."

And Arrol thought that his life was a very changeable color of events, each of them, good or bad, too precious in his memory to forget. And in the remembering each variation of memory could flicker by with fear and triumph sharing the same space. He thought how he had tried to extend the grasp of the men he commanded and order all the common affairs into a civilized and reliable whole. He decided that he had not wanted to be king, but had been called upon to fulfill the task and he, had reluctantly, taken the mantle and done what was needed.

"I dealt fairly with all and left with my own reputation improved while not destroying that of the man who remained. My courage was tempered with compassion and my true love for all things, up to fear and hurt. And now I am dead, a most despicable thing, where all I have gained for myself is the opportunity to battle for my own soul. I am a king of men. Why must I fall to this place and provide sport and entertainment with the choice of my eternity lying in the balance?"

And yet, he knew he must fight as there was no other choice before him. If he failed to take on the choice his accomplishments in life would fade and his memory of them would become useless in the huge swath of history still being made. He realized that his deeds were important for his time and place and actually quite pedestrian given the wide path of history. He knew that he had left few tales of his daring and no songs of his deeds that would live beyond him. And he realized that he had one chance remaining to add to his legend. One chance to carry his memory into the future or hold it in this Middle Kingdom with a flourish of his ancient daring.

"So a victory or loss will guarantee some measure of immortality and a myth, at least in part, of my own making, as I can only react to what others bring to me or throw at me. I will be either revered or wicked and evil."

And Arrol wondered how he could lose as he had been a fair and honest as any man, and his deeds did help those around him, giving longer life, more pleasant circumstances to all. And he wished the time he had would stretch and give him more conscious time with his own memories while he clung to the hope that victory would be his.

"In my soul I know of woe, of petty theft of a farmer and some lies to stir the souls of my charges. I was never malicious but I did succumb to the evils of inaction, allowing others to sweep events in my favor without stopping them and correcting any inaccuracies."

Arrol was thinking of his dearest Evelyn, who seemed to fall under his spell when she fell into the enchanted river. He had never given voice to the thought that she was enchanted by magic rather than himself and always wondered if the spell would wear.

He considered other deceptions but always knew his purpose within them was true and he was looking at the larger view of his life. He decided that he could not lament his actions with every peasant nor with his own wife as he had been true to both, doing his duty and his best to make their lives better.

And he used his thoughts to roll each concept, each moment, each conclusion around in his brain, looking at them from all angles. He could not reach another conclusion, that taken in sum, the true number of small indiscretions did not change the sum of his valour, and deeds of good. His brain poked through cause and effect, rarely thinking on a higher plain, wondering if his actions had always been true.

And as he considered his life a stab of light broke up his thoughts and a voice loudly rattled his resolve beckoning him to the fight.

"I trust you have prepared, and your thoughts of strategy will help you quell your fear. This battle will test all of you."

Arrol was led from the palace through a series of corridors down into a chasm and a wide pier on a river at its bottom. The river moved through the steep-sided canyon as did Arrol as he moved toward an island which split the river just before it plunged even deeper into an abyss. The river here was shallow as its force was divided though it churned in the shallows as it picked up speed toward the cataract.

The boat Arrol took glided silently through the water appearing to have no motive power. And as he looked about he saw another boat moving toward the island from the opposite shore in a similar glide though the rapids.

Arrol could see his opponent, clad as he except he had a broach which held his cloak clasped at the throat. As their boats touched ashore each attendant page gave an identical warning.

"Beware his tricks or you will be more than dead."

201

Arrol heard the warning but stared at his opponent trying to take his measure. While Pellas' voice had been strong and clear the page's words were twisted and abrupt.

Arrol took his leave of the boat with a nod but not breaking his view as doubts crept into his mind. The warning had hit his heart and he quailed inside thinking his conscience might be gone forever in short order.

As Arrol stared he tried to place the man but he could not. He stood facing away from him, broad shouldered, his stance as wide as his shoulders, and his eyes cast down and hands clasped behind his back in silent benediction.

The man turned to face him, breathed deeply and closed his eyes, hued as blue as the nymph who led him to Pellas' palace. Arrol stood oblivious, as the boats slipped back into the water though they seemed to float on air while they moved against the current back to the pier on the river's edge.

As the man turned to face him Arrol caught sight of the broach which suggested to him events of slaughter of armies and weapons he only dreamed about and victories of smashing overwhelming ease.

The broach was a stone of sorts surrounded by a wondrous lustrous metal and was intricately designed, with delicate folds, looking as a flower petal.

It was an heirloom, the sign of this man's command. But it was a sign of his family clan rather than the great armies he had gathered, and was a potent reminder of his fair hand and long life. Even this king had a malediction of lament, he was too easily swayed by his subjects claims of need and accepted their stories without question to the detriment of his kingdom, even though he knew that kingdoms cannot be operated by sentiment. And so this King Ilore found himself staring hard at Arrol, wondering which of them would remain to inspire their flock.

King Ilore was a gentle man and a peaceful king who took his patrimony but never had the heart to lead a charge or bring violence upon his enemies. He always tried to find justice in mercy and allowed those with anger to speak their views and make their arguments. His approach made for an uncertain kingdom.

King Ilore had held a sword on his throne, but it was bejewelled with rubies and diamonds. The ceremonial weapon fit his hand but he was clumsy with it. It felt heavy to him and he never was comfortable wielding it.

And the mantle of leadership rested upon him but it chafed, though such discomforts did not inspire him to quest but rather to find the path of ease in navigating each issue that was brought before him.

Ilore's hands were soft but his mind was quick and tempered truly by all the dealings he had with his subjects, and his ability to find pleasing compromise that satisfied all.

But despite his soft heart and honest ways, despite his defense of the weak, here he stood on an island in a river in a canyon above a cataract about to undertake single combat for his soul.

Though he was there without weapons Arrol spied a pair of throwing stones. He turned to bid the boat farewell and spun back to see his opponent doing the same. Arrol wasted nothing and stooped to pick up the stones thinking to maim.

He threw the stone without thinking anything but murder, as Ilore was still facing away from him. The stone flew to its destiny over Ilore's shoulder and splashed into the river, the echo a stab of action quite unexpected as Ilore had expected some formal start to the affair. The hard splash hit Ilore almost as if the missile had, and he was thrust into the fight.

He turned to eye Arrol and moved away from him buying time to think.

He saw that Arrol held another stone so he managed to keep his distance while looking for a similar weapon of his own. He scanned the island, a wedge of low sandy soil, the river flowing on both sides and one end as the edge of the cataract, falling endlessly into the void.

Arrol tried to maneuver Ilore into a pinch with the river at his back. But Ilore knew when Arrol would spring his throw and as he drew back his arm, Ilore filled his sight, shortened the distance and leaped to hand to hand battle.

They grappled looking for an advantage. Arrol knew instinctively his advantage was to be the aggressor and so he smashed his forehead into Ilore's jaw, causing Ilore to releasing his hold on him. Arrol rose quickly and with a vicious cry he aimed a kick at Ilore's prone form.

"You are not a fighter so you must be the owner of foul deeds in life. The ability to battle is a life force of justice brought down on your enemies and fuels success in your journey," said Arrol. "You are soft and fragile and must have long been an heir awaiting the crown in idleness before you became king. Once you acceded to the throne nothing changed as your dynasty was secure and peace your goal."

Ilore cowed to the barrage, still on his side but he never lost his wits, so as Arrol gained confidence as his opponent did not fight back, he lost his guard, stepped too close to Ilore who grasped his ankle and pulled hard, sending him sprawling backward to the ground.

"Perhaps I am unfit and soft but I will not give up. You just fell like a stone and methinks your head is made of the same stuff," Ilore said as he pulled himself up.

And he laughed as the heavy thud of Arrol landing echoed up the canyon. Arrol moaned in pain perhaps merely winded and surprised but Ilore was surprised by the amount of pain he had inflicted and considered it deeply rather than follow up by beating on the prone Arrol.

Arrol crawled to his feet and glared at Ilore, believing him to be far less than a match for his aggressive will and battle experience. He did have a niggling thought that the soft Ilore was a nasty opponent who would take advantage of things unseen. He moved away and circled his opponent, gaining strength and focussing his thought. And Ilore kept his back to the river, which was only a stride away, realizing that this Isle of Aaon was now the host to the battle between two ways of conducting one's life and the way they approached the unsavory or unfortunate events of their lives.

Then Arrol struck with a lunge at Ilore's chest but he was ready and was equal to the test, moving away, first moving straight back to draw him in, and then lunging aside and pushing the aggressive Arrol's body into the stream, where he lost his footing and fell with a splash, floundering to find his feet.

And Ilore leapt upon Arrol pressing his weight upon Arrol's arms and keeping his own upper body dry, for sodden arms would slow his reflex. He thought in a flash of the curiosity that such violence was necessary to protect his legacy of peace.

A sickly feeling ran up his arm to his heart, like a deep chill that would never warm. And still he held on keeping Arrol beneath the river's surface and waiting until he stopped struggling beneath him.

And feeling it wane he waited still and then rose on the spot, knee deep in the water, raising his arms in the air, a sign of victory but he was met with only silence.

And he wondered why everything was so quiet. How would victory be met?

The spectators who lined the canyon walls saw Arrol's body stir and rise from the churning waters. With his back to his opponent Ilore did not see that Arrol had played him as a possum and bore him hostile intent, doubly so now that he had managed to avoid his doom.

Ilore heard a splashing of the river and was shocked at Arrol's rise. He wondered how he had failed and it seemed destiny was mocking his wits and stripping his sense of merciful victory.

As Arrol approached him Ilore's will to win failed and he wondered if he could summon again the ability to kill.

Ilore backed away from Arrol's advance to buy time to think as he was still shocked and confused and could not regain his desire to battle for his own life.

He moved back, away from Arrol, more and more, tempting his fate as he approached without seeing the island's cliff side. He fixed his stare at Arrol firmly stalking him framed in the branches of the river. And Arrol thought briefly of stopping his advance to prevent Ilore from simply falling to his death and doom. Arrol wanted an honorable victory and he believed that simply pushing Ilore back until he fell was a trick not worthy of his fate.

His honour intact, he stopped his advance, but Ilore did not stop moving backward as fear flared in his eyes. He was resigned to losing as his one chance went astray and he could not summon the anger to battle further.

As Ilore approached the brink Arrol leapt, as Ilore's foot found empty space. He grabbed his cloak and arm and held him fast, "Hold on and help me help your cause."

But Ilore knew he could not win a physical contest and was resigning himself to hell, ready to cast himself into the chasm, pulling Arrol with him. But Arrol heaved and bent his weight back, unwilling to win victory by suicide.

With a mighty heave he pulled Ilore away from the edge and then walked away from his peer, giving him time to gather his wits.

"I seek an honorable resolution to this affair. My character demands that any victory that is mine be won with honor. Do not cast yourself away. Within these bounds heed my words and prepare to continue your defense."

"It would seem that defeat is my only choice, especially now that you have completed such an act of bravery and compassion." said Ilore. "Would I have passed the same test?"

This act of contrition weighed heavily on Ilore who promised himself that he would do the same thing should the opportunity occur. He considered briefly simply running to the edge of the fall and casting himself over. And while he thought of mercy Arrol was concentrated on how to win the contest, how he would remain as the only one on the island still living and his life long journey consecrated in his victory. Deep down he thought his action would count for him, if indeed this contest was a tally.

Both kings were battered but the contest was just begun with much laying ahead before the conclusion was reached.

Ilore shook his head to rattle his thinking and clear the apprehension that had welled up in his thoughts. Arrol faced him but was growing weary of the wait for a resolution.

A rivulet of blood ran down Arrol's arm, mixed with sweat and dirt and the water of the river still draining from him and his sodden clothes. His legs showed many spots where harm had come and his cloak was torn. His hurts had helped him to focus his mind.

And Arrol stared at his opponent trying to pick up some detail in his manner or something else to gain an advantage.

Fixing his gaze on the broach which held the tatters of his cloak in place and saw the detail in its art. And seeing for the first time he gasped at the bold relief on the locket. It was a horse standing still upon the plain, without saddle or bit or bridle. It was no ordinary horse, its curves and sinews, its markings made it unmistakably Garland, depicted in his youth.

It bore the strong bearing the haughty demeanor, the untapped power but this horse was coloured gold rather than Garland's predominate grey.

And near this horse stood a spear, a lance in a spray of light, with a particular notch in the shaft. Endurendil it was, his very own scepter, his weapon of magic which defended him through his early tests of fate.

And Arrol was amazed and then angry that Ilore would choose to turn these symbols against him. And while he turned this chance over in his mind he looked at Ilore's bearing, and took stock of his wounds and hurts. Most were confined to his torso including a deep cut that oozed blood from his hip. His face was pale as if the blood from it had gathered and collected at the places he had been cut, bruising his face and giving it a few streaks of blood.

Crouched like a dragon, Arrol stood up and relaxed his stance and upon seeing Ilore do the same, he charged. Ilore was taken in by this ploy, but Arrol believed it within the bounds of propriety and was happily back to the fight without cease.

Arrol leaped upon his prey, like an animal without conscience just giving into instinct in a violent rage, tearing and hitting without cease. Anything that did not give Arrol a chance to destroy was punished and used against his enemy. Grass was torn and thrown in his face, small stones were ground into his body by his height or through the heel of his hand.

Arrol's wrath knew no bounds as he raged weaponless, using everything at his disposal as a potential aid. He had even used his possum time in the water to feel for any rocks hidden under the surface of the stream, but found only sand.

And more blood dripped from Ilore, soon forming a smudge where he stood. And Ilore fought back, but in a defense that was all a moment late, reacting to what had happened rather than what would. His hands were bloody and he wondered if he would ever be able to get the stain off them, or if it would even be necessary.

Arrol's fury ran thin as his energy dimmed and Ilore tried to get up but he fell back his body damaged and rent. And as he reached back to cushion the fall, his hand fell upon a small rock hidden by the sand, and closed around it. Arrol regained his breath and went in for the kill, and as he approached close quarters Ilore pushed the rock, almost like a put, still in his palm, as violently as he could, into the face of his attacker. And the force of the blow caused a strange sensation to course down Ilore's arm. Arrol staggered up straight and his life force began to pump through the wound caressing his face like a river delta. His life force was pumping out and he fell.

But with the blow, Ilore seemed to take strength, and once he was failing but now he got stronger.

"You are a fool and a loathsome creature of hate," said Ilore. "You deal with animals best, not men, as you fight to their code, even if you accede to a gentleman's decree. You look for every mode of battle but when you are handed victory, you hold back, because the mode of it would lend you too little honor and memory. Your approach is most inconsistent."

"And thou, who condemns me, who would choose to fight for their immortality when they had never lifted an angry hand except to stop their pain or save an heirloom? And what of the broach? You gained strength from it but I leap in where the powerful are too afraid and the powerless find fear and confusion. They fear for their deliverance so they find solace in other amusements. You who fights only in self-defense has left me gravely hurt but you have paid a high price."

"I lay in this pool of my own life force, which drains away leaving me pale and weary. But as I speak your own color changes and your orbs fix. Is it another of your tricks?"

And with that Arrol began to stagger with the weight of his body became too much for his soul, and his bloodied clothing adding to his torment. He could not think clearly and was like a man having drunk too much wine, and he waivered to and fro leaving a red tail of blood where he went.

He moved slowly toward the water and began to resign himself to his loss in this battle.

And Ilore sat up at the sight, "No!" he cried. "I am beaten and unable to defend myself or hide from you."

And Arrol fell without hearing. The splash in the shallows of the island, caused his body to roll over and his face pointed toward the firmament, as the current, bumping up against the island, slowly picked him up and floated him along with redness spreading around and coloring his journey.

The cataract, previously a light sound in the background of the battle, came forward in noise as Arrol's floating body neared its edge. The roar now drowned out any sound the beaten man might make.

As he approached the edge, Arrol slowly, weakly, raised his hand to the sky in a salute, a farewell, to all his dreams and hopes and schemes and he wondered at his failure his loss of eternal glory. And as he lowered his salute he thought of his life. He was not sorry.

He regretted nothing and had lived as he sought, making the choices he believed in and having a time of glorious passage. And he knew that his life would be a companion to those who fail but he would remain as the final victory to he who passes into joy.

And he realized that people like him, discreet in their actions and motivations, complete without moral purity but tempered also with justice and truth in full measure, were by far the standard of men.

He had sought his fate without words or favors and wandered through his life and its trail of destiny with his hope of being immortal in history. And with that idea fresh, the roar of the waterfall broke into his thought, near as it was. But he had no fear.

Ilore had dragged his broken body along the island, and was not far from Arrol as he neared the fall.

And he rejoiced at his victory, but felt his life blood draining away. He hoped that once Arrol's defeat was true that he would be delivered from his pains and perhaps the name of his opponent would shed some light upon the nature of the battle. He had to hold on until Arrol was finally gone.

Closer, closer to the edge Arrol drew as the river gathered its speed, and he knew solace for the first time and was content as he understood fully his own nature.

He wondered why he rationalized his actions, knowing he wanted to accomplish a thing but did not have the conviction in his heart it was right. The virtue of his choices was blinded by the chance of immediate gain and all the while he never took a wound, except in this heart.

He knew that if he had not such a division he would have laboured less in his life to cure the ills of good and evil, which cursed some adventurers but for others was their salvation and true calling.

Except for this deep demand of his soul his days would have been much different and perhaps his death would have been too.

A swallow in flight swooped through Arrol's sight and was clearly seen despite the growing gloom. The river quickened as it neared the edge of the fall where Arrol would be swept and finally lose his crown of ambition.

Feeling this speed Arrol cast his eyes back to the isle, for one last gaze upon Ilore to see if there was any reason they were cast together, the one remaining mystery in his existence.

The swallow found its way to Aaon's shore where Ilore thought it an omen, but fixed his gaze on Arrol's last, thinking the bird might be Pellas sent to heal his wounds.

"Come now swallow, the dire deed has been done and I have weathered the test and won. Reveal yourself and my opponent true, heal my wounds and take me to gain the promise of Pellas your king."

With that the swallow lunged at Ilore's head and removed his mask and carried it away without a sound, rapidly rising up the canyon cliffs.

Arrol watched the bird in its flight as it robbed Ilore of his anonymity and Arrol watched it go, realizing at the last moment that Ilore's identity was bared.

Arrol swung his gaze back to the island and in that terrible second where the water's momentum held him hanging above the fall, their eyes did lock and their stares melded before Arrol plunged for seven days and mornings, past a multitude of evil ways and warnings.

His last vision fixed in his mind forever now, unchanged, as he stared at a mirror image of himself, though deeply estranged from his own memories.

Ilore knew not of this revelation of perspective that Arrol had gained. And Ilore knew he had been a hair's breath away from the opposite fate but quickly dismissed the humble thought knowing he had triumphed in fame not infamy.

Ilore saw the wide-eyed shock of Arrol as he fell, but believed it to be the sign that he had found enlightenment in his fate rather than the knowledge of his opponent. And with Arrol gone, the firmament slid open and the stars shone into the canyon with Venus and Mars quite bright in their red and blue light. And the swallow swooped back dropping the mask into the river and alighted on Aaon changing into the form of the life giver Pellas. All of Ilore's wounds suddenly healed.

With his strength revived Ilore had risen to greet the swallow as it glided with only the barest wing beats toward the island. The bird was larger than distance suggested and as it reached the shore it flared its wings and turned into a man, landing softly on the island.

"I have been given the task to perform and speak at this test which brought you to this place where souls are purified. Departing souls must work to maintain the purity this test reveals," the voice rang loudly in the narrow canyon, as he spoke to Ilore and all those gathered to watch.

"It is said that every man enters and leaves this life with nothing, except the legacy they have wrought. With a family that legacy includes progeny, but even without, the legacy is large and the affect he has on others can be profound."

"With the knowledge of years he can pass his knowledge to the next generation extending his contribution for as long as anyone remembers him, and perhaps longer. Remember that few societies live eternally in the present, most are firmly rooted in the past, and allow the present to creep forward under the tutelage of those who curate the golden past.

"Those charged with leadership bear a similar burden as they are required to plant the seeds for the future to bloom and advise those around them what to expect when their time for leadership arrives. And so your legacy can be counted up, your virtuous deeds are yours alone as are those failings. It is the plight and curse of kings and haunts them, how do they balance the death which they will face with the life they lead that precedes it? The deeds of kings cannot hide among the mass of lesser men because they do not have foreknowledge of what they will face nor how to address it. They stand alone or they fall alone."

"Many men wish they could relieve themselves of the weight of all they came to be, simply by dying and moving on from it. But what would be the value of life if such were possible, where would your destiny lie?"

"And the crowning joy of a baby's birth, would have no meaning if life were valueless to our destiny. Those two who share that joy would know not the value of instant worth of new life. And the value of the direct heritage of a new life, the uniqueness of each of us would not exist, as we cannot seek it out."

And the man, now speaking more to the assembled and tortured souls continued.

"We all enter into life with much good on our ledger. And most of us do not know what goals we pursue nor why, but we should. People focus their lives on safety and security and ignore the pure wild call of their heart. They wander through wonder in futility never really finding the depths of their abilities. And in death we can lament this happen-stance, as in death it is sealed in its own history. And now you have seen the victory of one soul and you can help to save others from this fate of standing at the end for a chance at virtue that could have been gained in life, rendering this place unnecessary.

"Might you benefit from a dose of reality, a view of your future in youth. Greed nor gain for its own sake will not advance your life because you live in constant pain and fear. You can pursue whatever dreams may come, whatever your heart fancies or your imagination creates, thoughts beyond number and none of them encumber your ability to achieve."

His voice rang in the clear air and the man, transformed again into the swallow and Ilore too, left the island and flew. Only a bloody tattered cloak, rent with tears and cuts of violence lay forlorn on the sand of the strand. Yet that remaining tattered cloak was a symbol still of human spirit and will and remained on Aaon for future wanderers who wonder about their choices in death and life.

As Arrol fell he chanced upon the thought that he had finally found what he had always sought, he was finally conquered by his own choices and would arrive among other such souls taking a bit of joy in their own fatal flaws, with their minds clear and their unconscious fear of not knowing now past them.

"That I lacked a direction for my choices is clear, but now I know and I have that joyful knowledge of my failing and remain me, with my faults intact."

And Arrol's life flared across the heavens and flickered out of sight, leaving the sky without his light. The final flash of sight proved to him that the combatants could never be divided by the result of their battle.

Arrol had worked each of his days for immediate gain with no thought to the future or where his choices would lead him.

History will rot away, if in the future we exist in the present. And if our tomorrows are ruled by what we do now, then our past must have full knowledge of now and what has led us to now. It is the only way we can march boldly into the future with some certainty that we are on the right path.

*****

And all characters move through their lives confused by all the wonderment they encounter and wishing they understood the reasons, their hopes and dreams while they blunder at changes they do not understand all the while reaching for something above their station and almost invisible to their nature. Reaching for something they do not understand.

Reaching and striving, even without a clear goal, seems better to them than simply standing around waiting for things to happen. What they don't see, is that they are where they are by their own choices and they occupy their spaces because they are comfortable and happier to remain rooted than reaching without the knowledge of what they reach for. They reach for material things because they rarely consider that contentment of their minds and souls is far more important, even if most people avoid such choices because they are difficult.

And we all pay a price to learn our lessons in life, but that price is not constant nor assigned invariably to each person. Would that such lessons were tied to their value so that payment would cause no concerns. And experience can have a wide effect as those who passively witness it can also learn from it. Indeed, even the smallest of matters can be hugely important turning points which nobody sees as connected to future events. Some people make a thought, an aphorism, a motto, their abiding principle in their lives and believe their adherence to it is their shield, making them invulnerable.

*****

And the tale of one man is now complete.

However, those connected to him will ever believe that the tale never really ends it simply becomes more complex as it adds to itself the multiples of everyone and everything it touches. For Endell his choices affected Evelyn and Rodney and Kevin the most, but also every page, squire, farmer, yeoman, guard and all others whose path he crossed.

Everyone wants a piece of immortality, in the cry of a baby, the turn of a phrase, or a memorial stone under a fully grown tree. And yet it is true that immortality is wasted on the dead, who may have achieved it, but can never know of their success.

With nothing except ambition Endell grew into the noble Arrol, claimed the kingship and achieved wealth, power and courage, for which he was famous. He let nothing deviate him from his path to success and he gained the world that he sought, but did not save his soul. His quest for fame consumed the truth as he set it aside from his straight path to weave his choices and remain on his chosen course. His flame burned brilliantly for a time but it flamed out and is now only an ember, still burning in all those he touched.

All battles are laced with legendary tales, of courage, selfless bravery and heroes, many of which have travelled in death and not achieved their paradise as their memories of their violent achievements are not memories of joy.

And yet my toil at the telling of this tale is now done, as the story is finished. I am on to other work, other choices of where to place my own effort. I beg you to consider the story and allow me to escape without explanation of what this is or why it was written, and to move on from my own choice to tell it.

I hope readers, that you have enjoyed sipping this story, or gulped it in as you saw fit, and that it's style or approach did not hurt your sensibilities or tax your brain. I am hopeful that anyone who invested their time with this might find a line or a moment that might move them. Though I am fully aware that others will never approve the archaic style or imperfect patterns and thoughts. Some people would destroy the rhythm and rhyme as they believe it is unnatural and ridiculous rather than taking the joy from the effort necessary to create it.

It is obvious to all that everyone had faced temptation at some time and have wondered if they should commit a crime in their own minds or in the minds of god. This is true even of those who hold no god supreme, as everyone, as they plan their efforts and consider their choices, still pray for luck.

It would be a wonderful life to have an unblemished conscience on everything you have ever done or thought. But it is not possible as people by their nature must consider many things as possible even if they are not chosen. It is that dark side that we all have that leads some of us to bad choices and bad outcomes.

At the end of all, every soul has a portion of its existence to reconcile, to forgive, to explain away, because you cannot destroy your own self - you cannot chose evil, you have to justify it as not being evil. And in the end your soul will define what is legitimate and just because without free will in the matter we are only dust.

The End

Taken from the novel

'A Picture of Distance'

© F. Bradley Reaume

Chas looked at himself in the mirror on his way out the door. Not quite the same 21-year old he had been 40 years before. As he continued his gaze he realized that exactly 40 years ago he had been struggling trying to salvage the engine of a Spitfire that had been hit by anti-aircraft fire during the D-Day invasion.

Walking the beaches now 40 years later lost in his thoughts for the last few days, Chas had enjoyed the time with old mates and his brother Bill. He kept straying to thoughts of Ver Sur Mer and his friend, the pilot Gordon McAuley.

He had written many months ago to The Caen War Memorial to get information on the museum for his trip and inquiring after the final resting place of Bill's friend Frank Edwards and his own wartime acquaintance Simon MacDonald. The museum put him in touch with a Jacques Gaspareau, a member of the French resistance during the war and a local historian.

Mon. Gaspareau wrote back saying that he did indeed know the spot where Lieutenant MacDonald was buried as he had been on a patrol that day in 1944 with his Resistance fighters when he came upon the body of MacDonald. He said the resistance often came across Allied soldiers and secretly buried their bodies to keep them out of the hands of the Nazis who were known to take out their frustrations on the corpses or otherwise denigrate their service.

Mon. Gaspareau said he would be happy to escort Chas to the site and show him around the area.

Chas remembered the events that led to Simon MacDonald's death. He had known Simon as a fellow mechanic. They had become friends as Simon was from the small town of Streetsville, just west of Toronto.

Only a few days after the D-Day landings, with the mechanics busy keeping the landing forces mobile, there had been a late afternoon call from Division for a mechanic to go to the recently seized bridge head outside of Reviers.

Chas was head deep in an engine just as the message arrived. Simon was just making the last few turns with his wrench to finish up the job on his vehicle. He volunteered.

Chas only heard of the events of that day from some of the other boys he had contact with. Simon never returned. When Simon arrived the Germans were apparently in retreat and many Allied tanks and personal were across the river. So Simon ran across the bridge without too much concern to reach a tank that had stalled and partly blocked the bridge egress.

According to those who witnessed it, a squadron of German fighters swooped down on the bridge at that moment and strafed the column trying to squeeze around the stalled tank.

Simon was hit multiple times and knocked off the bridge and into the river. In the chaos of the battle, and not really knowing that Simon was officially there, he was overlooked until several days later when he did not return to the motor pool.

Inquiries provided the story and likely end of Simon MacDonald. His body was not officially found until the burial spot was disclosed after the war. French partisans, including Mon. Gaspareau, found him down river and buried him in a quiet place without much ceremony.

After the war they provided his dog tags to officials who were able to match him up with their records and officially record his burial place. Normandy is dotted with these types of graves, usually unobtrusive, peaceful and enough out of the normal ebb and flow of daily life to be almost forgotten.

Chas was pleased that his inquiries were able to produce MacDonald's final resting place and a guide to help him find it.

Chas called Mon. Gaspareau. Thanks to the Frenchman's very European ability to speak more than one language they were able to quickly agree to a time and place to meet. Chas gave his full name to Gaspareau and began to spell it but Gaspareau stopped him.

"No, no Charles. Stuart is a well-known name around here," said Gaspareau.

Chas expressed surprise. "Oh, well, then I needn't spell it for you. I'll be with my wife. How will I know you on the platform?"

"Do not worry monsieur I will know you – what tourists we get in Ver Sur Mer usually come by car. You will be well known to me on the train platform. I can spot a tourist anywhere," he laughed.

As he hung up Chas smiled at the thought that Mon Gaspareau could see through his attempt to be more restrained than the average tourist.

"It's the running shoes, dear," said Anne, who had been eyeing him eyeing himself. "They give you away, that and the Toronto Maple Leaf jacket you've been wearing. Honestly, even with a few more cameras around your neck, a tour book in your hand and a map in the other you couldn't possibly look more like a tourist."

"At least they don't mistake us for Americans," he said.

"But they do. And if they don't it's because of the jacket dear, not because you don't look the part."

They ambled out of their hotel room in Caen and made their way to the train station where they boarded the train for Ver Sur Mer. Securing their tickets they settled in for a 30 minute ride. Stopping at a number of village cross roads the train never worked up much speed. Soon it was slowing again as they reached their destination. A few of the passengers began to gather their things to disembark. Most appeared to be going on to Bayeux or Cherbourg. Chas and Anne would return to Caen that evening.

The train pulled into the station and it was immediately obvious there was a major ruckus occurring on the platform. It was raucous and crowded. And what first appeared to be some sort of trouble, soon looked more like a huge crowd awaiting a movie star or something.

"There must be a movie star or singer or some celebrity on this train. Listen there's even a band out there."

"Perhaps if we moved up the train we'll get clear of all the commotion. I don't even know what Mon. Gaspareau looks like. I bet he was counting on a quiet day on which to find us."

So the two Canadians moved through a few cars trying to clear the crowds.

Chas saw a young man trying to manoeuvre a large box through the now open door. He was carrying a television camera.

"Here, I'll give you a hand with that," said Chas picking up the equipment box and moving through the door onto the platform, saying over his shoulder, "You'll miss the big moment if you don't hurry."

As Chas emerged, the platform erupted in a big cheer. He looked down the length of the train trying to catch a glimpse of whoever the big star was that everyone was waiting for. Anne stepped off behind the camera man who struggled with his rig.

Chas looked at all the people to see what they were focussed on but they were all seemed to be looking at him or the cameraman. The band struck up O' Canada.

Everyone seemed to have a Canadian flag, and a banner was unfurled from the facing of the station wall, which said "Bienvenue, Charles Stuart, Hero of Ver-Sur-Mer.

"What? There must be some mistake," he said to everyone and no one in particular.

A man appeared at his side.

"Monsieur Stuart, welcome to Ver-Sur-Mer, or welcome back for the first time in 40 years. When Mon. Gaspareau told me you were coming, well, I was overcome with joy. Your efforts to save our town and your extraordinary bravery to alert Mon. McAuley to our need will never be forgotten. This station is named Gare McAuley and the street on which it lies is Rue de Charles Stuart."

And so Mayor Jacques Martin of Ver-Sur-Mer directed Chas and Anne down the platform and through the cheering crowds of people. It appeared as if the whole town had turned out for the event. Every child was in their Sunday best, the boys with ties and the girls with flowers in their hair.

Down Rue de Charles Stuart they marched with a band keeping the beat alternating between Le Marseilles and O' Canada. People hung out their upper windows of the small central section of town, straining over the flower boxes to see the parade. In the midst of it all was a still bewildered Chas who wanted nothing more than a quiet afternoon in a small French town. He had come prepared to mourn his comrades.

At the end of the street was an open square with a dais to which Chas and Anne were led. Beside the square was a neatly kept cemetery with rows of white tombstones and a number of larger stone monuments. A small group of war graves were clearly visible from the platform decorated with national flags.

Several dignitaries were seated on the platform and all, save one older man, rose as Chas and Anne ascended the steps.

"Bonjour Madames et Monsieurs," Mayor Martin boomed before switching to English. "I have often longed for this day – to finally have the chance to thank our liberators for their bravery – face to face."

"On that fateful day I was a young boy living on Rue Esmerelda," he waved off to his left and explained for Chas his story as many in town were already familiar with it. "Just over there about a block from the bridge over La Provence. The Canadians saved my life, my family, my town and our beloved France."

Mayor Martin paused remembering a few fateful moments that made up most of his wartime remembrance. A tear gathered in the corner of his eye.

He remembered the day . . . .

"A Picture of Distance" is the story of three generations of the fictional   Stuart family of Toronto. Beginning with their matriarch and ending with her death at nearly 100 years of age, it is the story of the 20th century seen from Canadian eyes.

An excerpt from the novel

"All Fall Down"

© F. Bradley Reaume

Three crew members exited the bridge
and made their way quickly into the hold.
Under a large hatch they made their
mechanism ready. One of the crew went
immediately to a large cylinder perched
on a cradle. He fiddled with controls embedded in it and then patted it, before
moving away.

The Sea Merchant continued on the path
set by the now dead pilot moving through
the Upper Harbour between the Statue of
Liberty and Governor's Island towards the middle of the Hudson River. It
cleared the southern tip of Manhattan.

The captain had increased the ship's speed to maximum and the ship churned
against the current, making its way remorselessly up river. Minutes passed.

The radio crackled to life.

"Sea Merchant, you should be reversing engines to initiate your move to
stern. Report."

The captain let the message repeat twice before picking up the radio.

"P-72, we have radio problems. Your signal is not clear. Is it time for reverse
engines? Please confirm."

The captain reached for the controls and pressed a button which set the hold
cover in motion, once engaged it would open up the cargo bay exposing
machinery stored under the deck. The whine of the motors hauling the heavy
metal cover away from the large opening in the deck could be heard throughout the ship. Several more minutes passed.

The Sea Merchant had cleared the tip of Manhattan and was passing the
North Cove Yacht Harbour.

An explosion on the bow stunned the ship. Small explosions and shrapnel ripped through the bridge followed by a roar of jet engines. Two F18s flared out over head, now visible through the shattered glass of the bridge as they made their way up the Hudson. They made to turn for a second pass.

The captain grabbed the internal radio control. "Fire!"

The F18 pilots had located the ship, their first rocket had hit the bow in an attempt to disable the screw. As they passed they saw the opening in the deck. The fighters fired their first close range volley into the control tower to attempt to kill anyone there and further disable the ship. Two Port Authority speed boats were making their way to the Sea Merchant as the jets passed overhead.

Since Rome and the near miss in London the previous year, western port operations were sensitive to anomalies in procedure. The F18s could be on scene within minutes of getting the call. Other defensive measures were also engaged.

The jets wheeled around to challenge the tanker ship again. Both pilots expected to again pepper the control tower, and then swing around to fire rockets at the screw, just under the waterline in the stern. However, both pilots had seen the open hold and the strange contraption inside.

"Shit, Red Leader what was that?" the question was unnecessary as both pilots knew what they faced.

They had to target ship's command and the hold on their second pass. They made calibration adjustments as they turned to bear down on the Sea Merchant.

The planes took deadly seconds to turn around. As the fighters approached the ship, the large metal cylinder in the hold was flung skyward by the contraption it was resting in. The first F18 pilot couldn't target it as he was locked in on the ship and was too close to recalibrate his target. He fired anyway, as he had no other shot. Two rockets exploded against the bridge and two more entered the hold area.

The rockets hit amidships, into the open hatch and exploded convulsing the deck. A small dingy was nestled under the ship's port side and a few men had jumped aboard. Red Leader had seen the men flee the tanker and wondered for a moment what they were doing.

A Port Authority speedboat approached the Sea Merchant and shots pinged off their boat. They returned fire to the deck edge of the ship and swung around the larger cargo ship to see men boarding the dingy. They squeezed off a few rounds before more shots came their way, causing them to duck and take cover as they rounded the bow.

The second fighter pilot was also targeted on the ship but with more time to react as the cylinder rose he flipped quickly to manual and let off a stream of rounds aimed at the cylinder as it climbed into the air. His desperation, coupled with the speed of his jet and proximity to the new target guaranteed his miss.

The metal cylinder, about seven meters in length, and not quite two meters in diameter, glinted in the sun as it slowed, reaching the height of its upward thrust. It looked like someone had flung a piece of sewer pipe into the air.

Some New Yorkers with a view of the river watched the dance between the jets, the ship and its cargo with only the faintest idea of the drama was occurring. A few knew what they watched and simply held firm, unable to take their eyes off the drama. Most New Yorkers only heard the sounds, which reminded them of the September 11th airplane attack.

The cylinder hung over the river, pausing briefly as it lost the last of its upward momentum and began to fall back to earth. The second F18 pilot exhaled as he banked his plane over the Statue of Liberty and turned towards the Jersey Shore, now two miles away from the river, then three, then four.

The Red Leader F18 pilot had banked the other way over Brooklyn and had turned back toward Manhattan when a sunburst filled his screen. He was flying at nearly the speed of sound directly into a nuclear fireball. He pulled on his controls in a hopeful but ultimately inconsequential attempt to survive.

The second pilot was moving away from the explosion when he saw the flash of light coming from behind. He continued to fly away from the scene waiting for the inevitable shock wave.

As the cylinder rose against the backdrop of Manhattan, the crew screamed "Allahu Akbar". The captain clicked off a text message . . . "It is done." As he pressed 'send', the bomb exploded.

The presence of fighter jets had alerted many New Yorkers to the drama in the Hudson. Many thousands could see the ship and witnessed the attacks from the fighters. Many saw the cylinder rise from the ship and could feel their chests tighten - not really knowing why, but fearing the worst.

The cylinder had reached just over 400 feet in altitude, falling back about 35 feet before exploding. Watching from the upper floors of many Manhattan skyscrapers the skirmish on the Hudson was small and far away given the vast scope of the city spread out beneath them. The cylinder reached up only as high as some of the smaller skyscrapers in its vicinity.

Millions were vaporized as the air itself burned. With temperatures rivaling the center of the sun, metal and glass melted, the water in concrete and mortar boiled and exploded. The air itself was consumed with the resulting shock wave, first pushing everything outward and then rapidly pulling it back in as the air itself rushed in to replace that which was consumed.

The southern half of Manhattan was utterly destroyed. The huge buildings were shattered and tumbled like children's building bricks and what wasn't vaporised was pushed into the East River. Buildings provided a backdrop against which the shock wave pushed and the rubble piled up against rubble. The southern tip of Manhattan was stripped clean. The built up section of the Jersey shore suffered the same fate.

In Mid-Town, Brooklyn and the further Jersey Shore the stripped land gradually gave way to rubble and remains, with construction materials pummelled, crushed and pushed out from the center of the blast. Temperatures set everything on fire with much of the fire damage confined to the fringes of the damage zone leaving Queen's, Brooklyn and large parts of Bayonne, Jersey City and Union City a raging inferno quickly devoid of most of the millions who had lived there.

"New York control to Delta 455 we are handing you over to the JFK Tower - on Radio five - zero -niner. Safe trav . . . "

"Oh my," said the Delta captain as he saw the flash wash across his windshield from the south of his plane's approach. He signalled his co-pilot, "Raise New York control." He began a turn to the south.

"New York this is Delta 455 we just saw a huge flash . . . oh my God," he trailed off, the beginnings of a mushroom cloud were rising in the distance.

"Try them again and if there is no response try JFK."

"All Fall Down" is a story of a nuclear terrorist attack on the United States and the aftermath as issues of revenge, justice, economics, and politics all converge to create a new future.

From the novel

"Casting Giant Shadows"

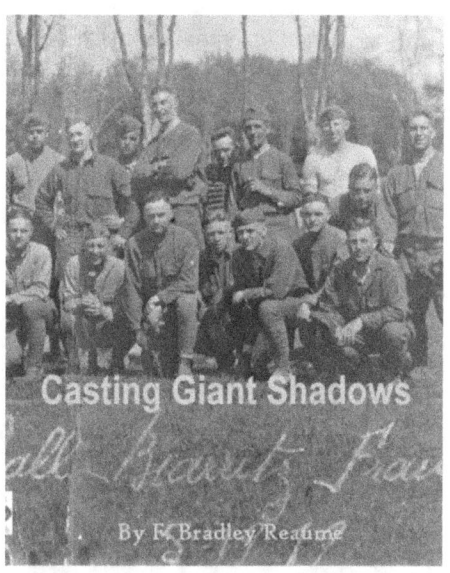

Casting Giant Shadows

By F. Bradley Reaume

© F. Bradley Reaume

The troop ship sailed triumphantly into New York harbour, sounding its horns, with the deck full of happy soon-to-be ex-soldiers. Fire boats launched a celebratory spray into the air. An unflappable Lady Liberty watched the joyful proceedings.

The ship docked and disgorged its passengers to a general liberty. A formal leave taking would begin the next day and the ship would remain in New York as a floating hotel for three days while all the men made arrangements to travel from New York to their home towns across the country. Eisenrick invited the platoon to his family bakery early the next day before they all began to get shipped out the following morning.

"I won't pass that up, Frankie," said Jocko Rollins. "I'm guessing your mom makes better stuff than you. I'd like a little bit of heaven before I head home to Missouri."

Momma Eisenrick faced quite a sight at precisely 0-800. She had just completed the rush of morning orders and was standing behind the counter with her head down, thinking of her next task, when a noise caused her to look up from her ledgers as she was reorganizing her mind for the morning.

The boys worked it perfectly. The entire platoon entered the bakery by the front customer entrance, filling the small sit down area where croissants, bread and pastries were sold to walk-in customers each morning. There was a huge hubbub of noise and confusion as they all piled in, much to Mrs. Eisenrick's amusement and consternation. She knew a troop ship had landed the previous evening, in fact it was a regular occurrence.

She put her index fingers to the sides of her mouth and whistled loudly, instantly quieting the hubbub. "What can I get you boys this morning?"

Clancy chimed up, speaking his lines, "We're looking for Frankie. He promised us a bun, like he used to make us in France."

"Oh, you know him? I'm afraid my Frankie hasn't arrived home yet," she said with a sad shake of her head.

Then the door to the ovens behind the counter burst open.

"Momma, momma, I see you've met my friends," said Frankie, who had quickly snuck in the back way through the delivery doors and donned an apron. "I promised them an Eisenrick apple pastry for bringing me home safely." He smiled a huge smile.

His mother began to shake. Her eyes welled up with tears which rolled down her face as her feet were rooted to the floor. The room was silent. Her legs felt like over cooked spaghetti.

"Oh Frankie, you're home, you're safe and you're whole. And you promised pastries to these boys for brining you home. That's all?" She threw her arms around him and hugged him tight, but only for a moment to make sure he was real. She caught herself, wiped the tears from her eyes and cheeks and mastered herself to take a stern look at her son.

"That's all? She grabbed trays of pastries and put them up on the counter. Please, eat. Everyone of you, eat with my thanks for bringing my boy home safely."

A huge cheer went up and Mrs. Eisenrick hugged Frankie again, all the harder.

"Fire up the ovens we are going to need another round of morning pastries," she yelled into the back part of the shop, always the pragmatist. The pastries disappeared in moments so more croissants found their way from the ovens and were offered and then bread was cut, slathered thick with butter. The late morning orders would be a bit behind that day.

"What's all the commotion?" asked a greying man, coming through the oven entrance to the sales area. He was wearing a heavy coat, fresh back from deliveries.

He spied Frankie still being clung to by his mother.

"Father, I am home."

The elder Eisenrick took a step back, blinked a few times and then flung his arms around his son's head. "Safe, as I always knew you would be." He recovered himself quickly. "When can you start delivering for me?"

Everyone laughed.

The Eisenrick's afternoon customers received their orders a bit late that day, but not one was upset once they were informed of Frankie's return. He was well known to their customers.

The next day as they left the ship, the Eisenrick's had made sure that every member of Frankie's platoon took with them a fresh loaf of bread and a bag of pastries for their journey.

One by one the platoon members took their leave, most bidding farewell and reminding each other of their promise to their Captain to meet again in 10 years.

"Casting Giant Shadows" is the story of an American platoon serving in France in World War One and their friendships and lives after the war.

An excerpt from

"Past Immortal As We"

© F. Bradley Reaume

"Okay, sorry about that, I have too much to think on. I have an exam in particle physics tomorrow and I brought my notes to review while I'm here."

"Ethan?"

"These exams are murder. First thing in the morning, I'm a mess, can't think straight until at least noon. At least it all makes sense, even if the details sometimes elude . . ."

"Ethan?"

"Yes John, what is it?"

"Take a look for yourself," John Overholt was standing in front of the desk and gestured down to the terminal in front of him. John's height lent him an air of being a bit laconic most times. He would never have interrupted even a wait-ress reciting the daily specials, and his interruption caught Ethan.

With a quizzical look on his face, which consisted mostly of a wry smile and severely crinkled eyes, Ethan moved to the desk. He was shorter than John, though pretty much everyone was shorter than John. He had dark hair which he wore a bit longer than most and combed back with only the slightest touch of gel. Jeans and a button up, collared shirt completed the graduate student ensemble.

"Don't tell me a gremlin got into the data sets. Have you gone and physically looked at the dish to see if it is working alright?"

"A gremlin, that's it. A gremlin that can multiply prime numbers."

Ethan's gaze narrowed. He moved his shorter body to the chair and slid in. He focused on the screen. He was silent for a long while.

His voice was quiet, "I take it you've checked for anomalies? Checked for computer function, the electronics and checked the array? Overholt nodded.

Ethan hadn't taken his eyes from the screen.

"That pretty much settles it. First Contact. Now they'll pull our SETI money."

Overholt couldn't help but laugh. "I doubt that. But I do like the fact that you have made First Contact, the most momentous moment in human history, all about you."

Harendez smiled. "No matter what happens, it's always all about me. The world laps its waves on my shore; I got that from a poem somewhere."

"It's nice to know that the liberal arts have had their impact on even the most cynical science student."

"Let's not take too much of a leap. I think I read it in middle school."

"Apparently your most productive education. And what else have you retained from those halcyon days?"

"I can multiply. So, thinking on it again, now I think they'll double our SETI money. First Contact leads to two way communications and then eventually a face to face visit. Right?"

"First Contact Ethan. Let's just take our time on this one. Unless I miss my guess, these signals seem to be coming from an Earth-like planet about 5.5 light years away. Close cosmologically but still a bit far for us to travel to easily."

"Who are they? What do they want? What does this number sequence mean?"

"I'm glad you asked," said Overholt. "So I will tell you. I have had several hours to puzzle it out."

Ethan's eyes went wide. Overholt stared at Ethan, preparing to speak, but didn't. Ethan looked at Overholt's forced bovine calm and they both began to laugh.

They laughed loud long and nervously, realizing as they did, that they were at the center of a maelstrom of publicity and science which would wash over them, consume them and spit them out very much changed, as the astonishing news spread.

For now, they alone knew the future. It wouldn't stay that way for long. Knowing the report would generate a call from the Head of the Department, a nano-second after he read it, John waited at the array, enjoying the effect his news would have on his supervisor, the President of the University and everyone as it rippled out across the whole world. He texted Allie, wanting her to know but swearing her to secrecy.

And Ethan couldn't stop talking about the inevitable media interviews, and practicing his responses. And they laughed and laughed, giddy at the sudden ridiculousness of it all.

"Past Immortal As We" is a science fiction story about First Contact with an alien intelligence and how humanity copes with the rapid changes in its foundations.

Excerpted from the novel

'Becoming'

BECOMING

BY F. BRADLEY REAUME

© F. Bradley Reaume

"We are staying on I-95 South so just follow the signs. We might be catching the back bit of the morning rush."

The highway snaked through some neighbourhoods, with highways, arterial roads and local exits every half a mile or so. Andrew watched, intently scanning the traffic and the overhead signs, smoothly swinging through the traffic. As the river harbour became more evident to their left, the traffic noticeably thinned giving them a whoosh of freedom as they crossed a bridge which gave them an unobstructed view of the harbour and downtown Jacksonville.

At that moment, three fuel tanker trucks were moving south of the harbour on the east side of the river.

"Holy shit," yelled Andrew a huge plume of fire exploded around either side of the elevated roadway. He mashed the brakes and wrenched the wheel to the right steering into the shoulder to avoid the pick-up truck in front of him.

The car behind him skidded and with nowhere to go, almost stopped before sliding with a crunch of metal into the pick up that Andrew had avoided. Cars and trucks in the left hand lane followed a similar trajectory, with some vehicles angling into the left shoulder, some being pushed into the guard rail and others pan-caking into each other to avoid the carnage.

A couple of fearless, stupid or slow to react drivers slipped through the fireball, either as they had no choice or because they had a clear path with fire towering over either side of the road.

The third tanker truck had driven at speed into the other two, stopped at a light under the highway bridge waiting for the green to continue southbound on the local streets.

Andrew and Diane said nothing as they both assessed the very slowly unfolding scene. A few hardy or crazy souls saw an opening, dislodged themselves from the mass of stopped vehicles and shot forward through the flames and smoke to the safety of the now empty highway in front of them. On the right shoulder, Andrew and Diane were blocked from moving forward by other cars that had become entangled or damaged in the rush to stop.

"You okay Diane?"

"Um, um, yeah. I'm okay. You?"

"Fine. Thankfully we avoided any collision. We can't go until those cars in front of us move. We weren't hit. I'm going to check."

Andrew flicked the latch and quickly got out of the car. He could feel the heat of the fire. A few of the other vehicles were spitting out people, most of whom looked awe struck at the flame perhaps 50 yards in front of them. Some scanned for damage to their own vehicles. The guy in the pick-up was near the back of his truck and looking at the woman in the car which had hit him. The damage to his truck was minor but her car's hood was folded and the front lights and grill were in pieces strewn across the pavement. She waved she was okay but was struggling with the door which was jammed.

The flames and smoke roared and rose with the sound of sirens somewhere off in the distance. Andrew could see the accident scene on the highway was only a few cars deep, as the thinning traffic had allowed those back of the accident to stop before crashing. As traffic had been thin on the south side of downtown, there were no serious collisions, just some twisted metal and jumbled vehicles. There was no way to back out either. Despite avoiding the accident, he was trapped by it.

With nowhere to go Andrew then looked forward past the pick-up to see if it could move. Two vehicles ahead, cars were twisted sideways and the paint on their hoods was blistering off due to the heat. Andrew could feel it, like the sun beating down on you when you already have a sunburn. However, 50 yards back from the source it didn't seem dangerous. It was almost soothing in the early morning Florida sun.

Then he heard a crackling. Diane had gotten out of the car and was motioning the driver beside them to exit her car from the passenger side.

"I think we need to get out of here," said the driver of the pick-up. "I don't like that sound."

"What about the people in the front cars?"

"You saw the damage. Did you see anyone moving?"

"Diane, get back and move off the road, get down the embankment. I don't know but with the heat and the damage I don't trust our gas tanks. I gotta at least take a look at that front car."

"Andrew be careful." She was shaking as if she'd stepped into a deep freeze. Smoke billowed up from either side of the southbound road.

"Just a quick look."

Carlton ran off, using the cars as a shield. The heat had dissipated as the size of the flame was reduced and was bearable and the smoke drifted lazily off to the north east, but the fire still crackled out of sight beneath the highway, with a lick of flame occasionally becoming visible to those on the highway. Andrew did not know that while one of the tankers had exploded, two others were engulfed in the flame, full of gasoline and leaking badly.

He passed a car where two people had gotten out and he motioned them back. "Get back quick. If there's another explosion it'll burn here."

With a few athletic steps he was at the front car. Through the window he could see three people all unconscious and sweating. He banged on the window. Two adults in the front did not move, but a young girl in the back seat shook her eyes open. She pulled on the door latch and the door opened a bit but was stuck.

Carlton used his left hand to touch the outside latch, for a tiny moment. Even though it faced away from the flame the door was superheated as he expected. He yelled and motioned for the girl to use her feet to kick at the door. She was too spent to be able to put much effort in.

He heard a series of pops from under the bridge. He sensed he had to get away quickly.

He took off his shirt and used it as an oven mitt. He grabbed the latch with his left hand and reached into the slight gap where the door had almost opened and pulled quickly and as hard as he could. It moved but did not give way. The shirt smoldered and his fingers burned. He tried again with a last bit of effort as the billowing smoke had increased. Looking around he noticed emergency workers had moved far back of the underpass and were watching it from cover. He knew the fire below was not spent.

He yelled 1-2-3 and together he pulled, the girl pushed and the door popped open. He grabbed her by the wrist, pulled her from the car, threw her over his shoulder and ran back, scrambling down the embankment, gently placing her beside Diane.

"I think I should go back to get the others."

As he started to rise a tremendous explosion ripped the air, blowing flame and heat up and out from the lower roadway as first one tanker exploded and moments later the second followed. The roadbed convulsed and gave way.

There was a wave of heat and those down the hill cowered into the ground until the blast furnace let up with most of its fuel consumed.

Andrew looked at Diane who appeared to be alright, comforting a small boy with his mother. Andrew noticed that a bit of Diane's shirt had melted into her shoulder. He looked at it long enough to see it was only an inch long section right at the point of her shoulder. She had some light burns on her right arm and neck, but it looked like a moderately bad sunburn.

He reached to touch her and she winced.

"Don't. I'm okay but that blast gave me a singe. It felt like taking too long to light a gas grill. You know, the gas flash as the flame catches the excess gas? I think it burnt off some hair."

Sure enough there were little burnt hairs on her upper arm and evidence of some burnt hair around her ear. There was an ongoing series of pops as the flame licked the underside of the remaining concrete highway bridge. Water in the concrete was exploding into steam, and failed concrete was falling in bits and chunks from what remained of the road bed into the conflagration below.

"We need to move further away. We don't know what else is under there."

'Becoming' is the story of youths making the difficult choices necessary to face their futures. It focuses on players, coaches and the families attached to a minor professional baseball team as they face the end of the season and look forward to what comes next.

From the novel

'Reckoner'

At the bottom of the tower Terrence turned left. We followed. I noted this is where the manor made its first bend away from the front entrance. We followed, taking a side passage, then another, until I was quite lost. We eventually emerged in a wide hall, proceeded down it past one or two doors and then plunged into the room.

We entered the Billiard Room where we had previously been with the men of the household not more than 30 minutes before. The billiard balls were on the table in their rack, with a game apparently ended. The room looked the same as when I had left it, tables, a cart with food and drink, lots of chairs, a small library and trophy weapons displayed on the walls. A crowd of servants filled the room but no one moved or even spoke.

Seeing Terrence lead us in, they parted, drawing him into the room. As he moved in past a billiard table he gasped and immediately fell to his knees.

I was immediately on his heels so a moment later I saw. His second son Michael, lay splayed oddly on the floor. His pallor and obvious discomfort made him look dead.

However, it was the small, heavy hatchet protruding from the back of his neck, and the large pool of bright red blood which made the diagnosis complete.

Terrence reached for the hatchet handle.

Swizenstien gently took his arm and told him not to touch the scene. He raised Terrence to his feet, getting between him and the body on the floor, gently moving to escort Terrence out, as the man descended into a deep shock.

"Clear the room and summon the police," he whispered to me as he passed.

I immediately corralled one servant and asked that she summon the police quickly. She scurried off to complete her task, happy to have something to do.

Once Terrence was out of the room. I began to herd the onlookers to the door, explaining that we must preserve the crime scene. Once they were all in the hall, I asked who had found the body and indicated that anyone who had come upon the scene before the crowd arrived should speak to me while we waited for police.

It quickly became apparent that nobody had seen much. A few had heard a loud voice, others a deep thump, while anyone else merely arrived to an already full room of shocked staff drawn by the commotion.

The maid I had sent off returned saying the police were coming and other staff would bring them through the Manor.

"I just went into the room, to give it a quick straightening once your meeting was over with the boys," she said to me. "I was in there cleaning up cups and plates and putting food on my cart to be taken away when I moved across the room to investigate after seeing an empty spot in the display case."

That's when I saw Master Michael and what had happened to the trophy on the wall. The next thing I knew there were many of the staff there. Oh, my word. What has happened?"

Swizenstien walked back to us, without Terrence.

"I have committed Terrence to the family medical staff. The doctor is on his way. The Earl has been told and insists upon coming to see."

A doctor appeared from a doorway nearby, walking so fast he nearly ran. "Is there anything to be done? Anything?"

"By all means look Doctor, but unless he can be saved do not move the body." Swizenstien opened the door and followed the doctor inside. "Blood has ceased flowing from the wound."

I stood outside with the maid, standing guard, waiting for the Earl and the local police.

The Earl arrived first and slipped inside.

The police came a few minutes later, during which time the maid said she had heard nothing and assumed the meeting was over as she had seen several of the participants moving down the hallway, but wasn't entirely sure it was over until she listened at the door and there was no sound.

I remembered that Michael seemed to be waiting for everyone to leave so he could speak, I presume, to his elder brother Edward. It was pretty thin evidence and I had no idea if they had been the last two in the room as Theodore had left, and I recalled Titus was playing Edward in a game, and Markus making his way to leave shortly after we did with Terrence. That left Edward and Titus in the room with Michael and Thomas unaccounted for.

The police began taking statements and I heard Swizenstien outline what I had remembered. I merely piled on.

Police asked us back into the room to outline our seating arrangements and ask if any of the discussion was heated. One police examiner was taking measurements and examining the body and its position. Before he covered the body with a white sheet I had an extended look at it again, this time without the moment of shock upon first witnessing it. The hatchet was deeply embedded in the neck and had likely severed his spine, causing Michael's awkward position on the floor and killed him by asphyxiation as he was no longer able to work his lungs to breathe. The blood was superfluous.

Thus he must have been there for more than a few minutes when found as it takes time to die in that manner, I thought.

Pondering this I realized with horror that the hatchet was the exact one that Titus had showed me the previous day when demonstrating the weight of various weapons. It dawned on me that my finger and hand prints were all over the handle. And I remembered the odd way that Titus had taken the hatchet from me, with his hands only lightly holding it at each end as he placed it on its hooks.

"Sir," I loudly attracted the attention of the police detective. "A word please."

Stepping aside with him I lowered my voice, "I remember that I was shown

242

this weapon yesterday and held it by the handle to ascertain its weight compared to other weapons."

The detective's eyebrows raised ever so slightly.

"And you again are . . . ?"

"Trewilliger, sir. I am an associate of Mr. Swizenstien the Earl's solicitor. "The young man Titus, the Earl's grandson was expounding on the various weights of the weapons on the wall and used the hatchet as an example."

"What other weapons did you handle?"

"Only a sword sir," I looked at the wall. "I believe it was this one," I said pointing at a blade.

"Thank you Mr. Trewilliger. If there is anything else you can remember please let me know," he handed me a contact card.

"I'm going to have to ask everyone to leave the room now as we want to do a thorough sweep and fingerprinting of everything."

The Earl himself walked out slowly with tears glistening in the corners of his eyes. He told everyone present to go back to their duties and said that the family dinner was still on, though delayed now as the kitchen staff had prepared the banquet and everyone was still hungry despite the tragedy. He acknowledged the celebration of his birthday was likely more of a wake for his grandson.

Reckoner is the story of a young lawyer who is drawn into a battle between spirits and wraiths during the settling of a vast titled estate.

F. Bradley Reaume

Brad has written his entire career, first as a newspaper reporter and columnist, and then in the political and government realm before pursuing fiction.

"A Wander Within Wonder" has been reprinted from a folio printed in 2003 with some minor corrections. The prose version of the narrative is new to this edition.

Brad lives with his wife and children in Ontario, Canada.

Also by F. Bradley Reaume

Novels

A Picture of Distance (2014) - a family saga

All Fall Down (2016) - future history after a nuclear attack on New York

Casting Giant Shadows (2017) - story of an American unit in The Great War

Past Immortal As We (2018) - story about alien first contact

Becoming (2019) - baseball team players and coaches face their future

Reckoner (2020) - a neo-gothic story in which a young lawyer faces ghosts and wraiths and the nature of good and evil

Other Books

The Wonderful World of Wogs (2014) - illustrated for pre-schoolers

   *** As Brad Reaume / Illustrated by Nicole Flax

Other Skylines (2015) - collection of short stories

The Rhyme of History (2014) - current affairs